Michael Bond made the decision to become a writer while serving in the Army in the Second World War. In 1947 he returned to the BBC, where he had worked previously, and spent some years there as a cameraman. Paddington Bear was born after a shopping trip on Christmas Eve when he spotted a small, solitary bear in a large London store. Paddington Bear is now a household name, and the Paddington Books have been translated into over twenty languages.

Monsieur Pamplemousse ('The Gallic welcome of a kiss on both cheeks for a new detective' *Good Housekeeping*) was Michael Bond's first novel for adults. Such was the success of his inspired blend of comedy, crime and cuisine that a series of books followed starring Pamplemousse and his bloodhound Pommes Frites. *Monsieur Pamplemousse Takes The Train* is the tenth in the series.

Also by Michael Bond

Monsieur Pamplemousse Takes the Train

Michael Bond

HEADLINE

First published in 1993
by HEADLINE BOOK PUBLISHING

First published in paperback in 1994
by HEADLINE BOOK PUBLISHING

10 9 8 7 6 5 4 3 2 1

ISBN 0 7472 4408 1

Printed and bound in Great Britain by
HarperCollins Manufacturing, Glasgow

HEADLINE BOOK PUBLISHING
A division of Hodder Headline PLC
338 Euston Road
London NW1 3BH

CONTENTS

1

NIGHT TRAIN FROM ROME

Monsieur Pamplemousse spotted the hat first: a splash of red bobbing about amongst all the dark suits and overcoats entering *binario* 21 of Rome's Stazione Termini. He couldn't resist taking a quick photograph. The light was not all that it might have been and he held his breath while he pressed the shutter. It would either work or it wouldn't. If it did it might make a good cover picture for *L'Escargot*, *Le Guide*'s staff magazine: a change from the usual gourmet offerings.

He had forgotten how soberly people tended to dress in Italy; dark colours predominated. In much the same way he had been taken by surprise, as he had been in the past, when he arrived in Rome the previous afternoon and caught sight of the suburban balconies festooned with laundry hanging out to dry. If it wasn't laundry it would be people anxious to chat with their neighbours. In some ways it was as unlike Paris as it was possible to be. Parisians tended to keep themselves to themselves.

Steadying himself against the side of the waiting train, he pressed the shutter release once more for luck.

The girl was accompanied by two nuns in long grey habits, one on either side of her. From a distance it was almost like prisoner and escort, although there the resemblance ended. The nuns had their heads covered by black headdresses. It was hard to tell what, if anything, lay beneath them. Most policewomen in Rome seemed to wear their hair provocatively long, way below shoulder-length. Again, quite unlike their Parisian counterparts.

As the party drew near he moved forward to greet them, conscious that the eyes of the sleeping-car conductor were not the only ones following his progress down the platform. An American couple in the next compartment to his – a grey-haired man and his vastly overweight wife – peered out through their open door. Wisely, Pommes Frites, worn out after all the walking they had done during the past twenty-four hours, elected to stay on the train.

Raising his hat, Monsieur Pamplemousse mustered the little Italian he knew: not much more than the basic pleasantries – '*Buona sera. Per favore. Grazie. Prego.*' The nice thing about the language was that you could always make things up and the natives seemed to understand. '*Sì, signorina. Je suis il signor* Pamplemousse. May I take your valise?'

The girl handed it to him gratefully. As befitted a relative of the Director, it felt expensive. Not what one might have pictured of the average convent girl going away for the half-term break. It also weighed a ton. He could see why she was glad to get rid of it.

'I am Caterina.' She spoke French with hardly a trace of an accent, although the intonation gave away her Italian origins. That, and the dark, expressive eyes.

'My first guess was correct.'

She laughed as she followed his glance towards the accompanying nuns. Their faces remained expressionless. It struck Monsieur Pamplemousse that he was being quietly vetted. He must have passed muster, for a moment later, after a barely perceptible exchange of glances, one of them held out her hand. It felt soft and warm to the touch. He wondered why he should be so surprised. It occurred to him that he had never held a nun's hand before. It was withdrawn almost immediately, as though she were reading his thoughts.

'I trust you will both have a pleasant journey, Monsieur Pamplemousse.'

'*Arrivederci. Ciao.* I will take good care of her.' He found himself launching into another series of basic pleasantries, bowing his way out of the encounter as the two women issued last-minute instructions to the girl; more warnings than advice he fancied. From the tone of their voices it sounded as though Paris was beyond redemption: a place of perpetual sin.

'Phew!' Leading the way back up the *quai* he felt the girl relax. The face beneath the hat looked wide-eyed and innocent, as pale as the faces of the nuns had been, but the lips and the slight flare to the nostrils, suggested she had a wayward streak too; not someone to be trifled with if you got in her way. Black hair peeped out from beneath the wide brim of the hat. Undoing her top coat, she revealed a

3

dark blue skirt reaching to below her knees, and a matching jacket over a starched white blouse.

Reaching the door to their coach, he waited patiently while the conductor collected the girl's passport and examined her ticket, ticking off her name against his list of reservations. He handed her a customs declaration form and then stood back to allow them access. The American couple were clearly talking about them, trying to work out the relationship.

'Is it possible to make a reservation for the dining-car?'

'There is no dining-car, *signore*.'

'No dining-car?' repeated Monsieur Pamplemousse. 'But . . .'

He gazed at the conductor. It would be useless trying to explain that the main purpose of his travelling on the train in the first place was to report on the catering facilities. Useless, and against all the rules under which Inspectors working for *Le Guide* were expected to operate.

'There is a buffet car, *signore*, where they do a hot dish. It is three coaches down. But they do not take reservations. I will fetch you some mineral water if you like – once everyone has boarded.'

'*Merci. Merci beaucoup.*' Monsieur Pamplemousse resorted to his native tongue. He couldn't trust himself to deliver the right degree of sarcasm in Italian. It would probably be wasted in any language.

With a heavy heart he set off down the corridor, pointing out his own sleeping compartment as they went past.

Pommes Frites opened one eye and gazed benevolently, if noncommittally at his master's latest acquisition.

The girl paused and reached down to pat his head. 'You

should have ordered two bottles of mineral water. Never mind, we'll see if we can get you a doggy bag from the buffet car.'

Pommes Frites returned her gaze with loving eyes. Clearly he was dealing with a person who knew the way to a dog's heart.

Monsieur Pamplemousse suddenly warmed to her too. He doubted Pommes Frites' response at being presented with the remains of someone else's meal wrapped up in silver foil when he, too, had most likely been looking forward to dining in style. However, it was the thought that mattered.

'That is a nice idea, but it will not be necessary. Pommes Frites will have to take his place in the queue like everyone else.'

'He travels with you everywhere?'

'Everywhere,' said Monsieur Pamplemousse firmly. Carrying on up the corridor until they reached the girl's compartment, he placed her *valise* on the seat.

'I take it you would like to try the buffet car?'

'You bet. I'm starving.'

'The train leaves at nineteen ten. Shall I give you a call at, say, eight o'clock?'

'Seven forty-five sounds even nicer.'

'Seven forty-five,' said Monsieur Pamplemousse. '*Arrivederci.*'

'*A tout à l'heure, monsieur.*'

Retracing his steps, Monsieur Pamplemousse entered his own compartment. Catching sight of the American couple watching his movements via a reflection in the corridor window, he closed the door and settled back to scan through the various *Compagnia Wagon-Lits Italia* brochures contained in a rack above the toilet cupboard.

There being no restaurant car was little short of a disaster. A sign of the times if ever there was one. The Director would be furious when he heard. Or would he?

Monsieur Pamplemousse gazed out of the carriage window with unseeing eyes. The train in the adjoining *quai* was just leaving, but he scarcely registered the fact.

Wasn't the whole situation typical of the tortuous way in which things at *Le Guide* were so often arranged? The simple truth was, the Director hated being put in the position of having to ask a direct favour of a subordinate. It was always a case of taking a circuitous route up and down the byways and round the houses before entering his chosen destination via the back door.

If only he had come straight out with it and said: 'Pamplemousse, I want you to do me a very special favour. My wife, Chantal, has a *petite cousine* who is attending a convent school near Rome. She is coming to stay with us for the half term. She will be travelling to Paris on the night express and one reads such strange things these days. I may be old-fashioned, but a young girl by herself... Unfortunately both my wife and I are otherwise engaged. I am up to my eyes in work overseeing the preparation of next year's *Guide* . . . Chantal has to go to Digne to attend the funeral of an old aunt who has just died . . . perhaps you wouldn't mind escorting her?'

That would have been easily understandable.

Instead of which it had been: 'Pamplemousse, I have been giving the affairs of *Le Guide* a great deal of thought over the past few weeks and it seems to me that it is time we extended our horizons. We should not remain stationary, but we should move forward. Air travel is but one area we have neglected in the past. Railways are another. Perhaps we should also have a section devoted to the great trains of Europe ... *Par exemple* ... PAUSE ... *par exemple* the night train from Rome to Paris ... I believe it is called the Palatino. With this in mind I have made arrangements for you to do some preliminary field-work. Oh, and *en passant* it just so happens that a relative of Chantal's will be travelling on the same train ...'

He must have got someone to check the arrangements, but it simply wouldn't have occurred to him to come straight out with the simple truth: 'I'm afraid it is not quite like the old days, Pamplemousse. There is no longer a restaurant car as such. It is a self-service buffet car, but I am told the *plat du jour* is always heated.'

As had happened so many times in the past, Monsieur Pamplemousse had been caught napping. Halfway through the Director's discourse – the point where he had opened a second bottle of Gosset champagne (the Grand Millésime Rosé '82!) – he had even found himself coming up with other ideas. Cruise liners might be a rich field to research – Truffert would be a good candidate for the task – he had spent some time in the merchant navy. Then there were converted canal barges in the Midi catering for small groups of holidaymakers – that would suit Guilot – he liked the quiet life. And why stop there? Loudier was getting on in years. Why not 'Meals on Wheels for the Elderly' before he finally retired? Come to that, eating in a dining-car was a form of 'Meals on Wheels' – why not send Loudier instead?

The Director had not been amused by the suggestion.

Almost imperceptibly the train began to move. They were barely out of the station when there was a knock on the door. It was the conductor with his mineral water: *Effervescente naturale.*

Pommes Frites gazed mournfully at the bubbles as his master poured some water into a dish. Bubbles tickled his nose and it was not what he was used to. Monsieur Pamplemousse heaved a sigh. Something told him he was in for a bad night. He opened the door before the atmosphere became too oppressive.

And at the end of it all, where was he? Sitting in an overnight train heading back to Paris, acting as nursemaid to a sixteen-year-old.

Sixteen? That is what the Director had said, and there was no reason to disbelieve him. She seemed pleasant enough. But what did you talk about to a sixteen-year-old convent girl? Perhaps it was just as well he didn't have to sit through a long-drawn-out meal.

Wouldn't it also be true to say that it was a way of getting Monsieur Pamplemousse's services for free? Madame Grante in Accounts might suspect the worst when she checked his expenses, but she wouldn't be able to prove anything.

Anyway, who was he, Pamplemousse, to argue? Looked at in another light, it was an unexpected bonus. Travelling aboard a trans-European express still had an aura of romance about it. He glanced around the cabin. The quality of the workmanship and the solidity of the wood and the metal fittings reflected the lavishness of a bygone age. It might lack the smoothness of the TGV, but it was certainly a pleasant change from the hours he normally spent crouched over the wheel of his 2CV.

Rome had been another bonus. Arriving late the previous afternoon, he'd had time to explore the city. It was bathed in a golden light and stank of petrol fumes. Along with hordes of others he had paid his respects to the Church of San Pietro, seen and marvelled at the ceiling of the Sistine Chapel, walked beside the Tiber – dusty and disappointing compared with the Seine, gazed at the view across the rooftops from the balcony above the Piazza del Popolo, walked in the Borghese Gardens – counting the number of broken off organs on the statues in the Pincio area – breaking them off was apparently a popular local sport, sat on the Spanish Steps; in short, he had done all the things a good tourist should do and in a remarkably short space of time. Art Buchwald's four-minute Louvre wasn't in it. Above all he had eaten well. Now, like Pommes Frites, he was feeling worn out.

A motherly woman bustled down the corridor ringing a handbell to indicate the buffet car was open. It was another reminder of more gracious times; a pleasant change from the ubiquitous hidden loudspeakers bombarding passengers with endless announcements.

Closing the door again he unpacked his suitcase and after a quick wash and shave, made his way down the corridor to collect the Director's *petite cousine*.

Engrossed in his own thoughts, he was totally unprepared for the sight which met his eyes as the door was opened in response to his knock. It literally took his breath away and for a second or two he thought he had picked on the wrong compartment. Even Pommes Frites looked taken aback. Clearly he was searching his memory, trying to pin down where he had seen the girl before.

'You should have warned me.' Monsieur Pamplemousse gazed at the elegant figure standing before him, trying hard to make the adjustment: a quantum leap from the schoolgirl he'd escorted along the *quai* less than an hour ago to a *soignée* young lady of the world; a dramatic mixture of striking understatement.

'You approve?' Moistened lips parted in a smile which revealed the whitest teeth he had ever seen. Liquid blue eyes gazed into his. There was a momentary heady waft of perfume as she pirouetted gracefully on one high heel – a vision of loveliness; hair, released from the confines of the school hat, now hung loosely about her shoulders, a fashionably short, dark red dress revealed silk-clad legs which under other circumstances he would have been hard-put not to linger over. Her skin was firm and smooth.

The total transformation took him a moment or two to get used to. Everything about the girl had miraculously changed. She even looked taller. Her neck seemed longer, perhaps because the low-cut line of the dress was emphasised by a small gold cross hanging from a chain. Two small diamonds, one in each ear, matched a larger diamond in the centre of the cross. Make-up underlined the fullness of her lips; her cheeks were now the colour of a warm peach. Her figure . . .

Monsieur Pamplemousse pulled himself together. 'I think,' he said gruffly, 'it is time we ate.'

It struck him as he led the way along the corridor, that had the nuns been following on behind they would have been searching beneath their gowns for bottles of *sal volatile*.

Half expecting the buffet car to be crowded, Monsieur Pamplemousse was relieved to find there were still a number of vacant tables. All the same, he was conscious of the stares from other occupants as they made their entrance. Seating the girl at a table which was still reasonably isolated, and leaving Pommes Frites in charge to ensure it remained that way, he gathered up three trays and slid them in line along a counter beneath a row of stainless steel shelves and compartments, picking up cutlery and anything else that struck his fancy as he went along. It was assembly-line catering.

He recognised the woman who had gone past his compartment earlier ringing the bell. She was presiding over a cash desk at the end of the small queue. Orders for the main course were dispatched in ringing tones through an open doorway to her right. A framed colour illustration of a *steak garni* was fixed to the side of the carriage opposite the kitchen. He wondered if it was there for the benefit of the public or the chef. Time would tell.

Monsieur Pamplemousse called out his order, then waited patiently while those in front of him shuffled forward. A polyglot clientèle, both in speech and dress; jeans and open-necked shirts predominated, with here and there a more formal suit. There were exchanges in Italian, German, Swedish and English.

'Can't think where they're all going to at this time of night!' his old Mother would have said, using the tone of voice she reserved for those occasions when she mixed deep-felt suspicion with impatience at being kept waiting.

He wondered what she would have thought of Caterina. He felt sure she would have warmed to her. It would be hard not to. 'Nice, but not too nice,' would have been her summing up.

'*Oh, là! là!*' Seeing Monsieur Pamplemousse struggling with the trays, the Madame in charge abandoned her till for a moment while she helped him back to his seat, fussing over him like a mother hen. It was a little piece of French territory on wheels, presided over by someone who had it all organised. Paper serviettes were spirited out of thin air. Clucking heralded the arrival of the condiments. *Bon appétit*s floated down the carriage as she returned to her post.

'I think you have made a conquest,' said Caterina.

'Not as many as you have,' said Monsieur Pamplemousse, glancing round the coach. 'Besides, I think she is glad to hear someone speaking her own language. I doubt if she approves of other tongues.' He poured two glasses of Côtes-du-Rhône.

'You do not mind *vin rouge*?'

'I do not mind *vin* anything,' said Caterina.

She looked around at the other diners. 'It isn't quite what I expected. Do you think I'm overdoing things? Nobody else seems to have bothered to dress.'

'You are looking absolutely ravishing,' said Monsieur Pamplemousse. 'That is no crime. I doubt if there is a girl here who does not envy you, nor a man who would not wish to ride off with you on his white charger.'

Suddenly aware that another passenger seated on the opposite side of the coach was listening intently to their conversation, Monsieur Pamplemousse glanced across and looked the other up and down. Having registered pointed black shoes, polished until you could see your face in them, and what he could only describe as an old-fashioned dark pin-striped suit – he couldn't quite say why it struck him as old-fashioned, perhaps it was the cut, or the over-wide stripes – a white silk shirt, pencil moustache, thick black hair, brilliantined and brushed back – it somehow went with the suit – he formed what was probably a wholly irrational dislike of the man. 'Il Blobbo' would be a good name for him. The fingernails of the left hand, which was holding a small glass of colourless liquid – it could have been Grappa – looked freshly manicured. Eye contact was rendered impossible by virtue of a pair of impenetrably dark Bausch & Lomb glasses.

Monsieur Pamplemousse was irresistibly reminded of the famous anti-Nixon campaign slogan 'Would you buy a second-hand car from this man?'. The answer in the present case was most emphatically 'no'. From the studiedly insolent way in which the other took his time before seeking shelter behind a copy of *La Stampa*, it was clear that the feeling was mutual, although he hoped it was for a different reason.

'Pardon?' He suddenly realised the girl was talking to him.

'I said, *grazie*. It is always nice to have compliments.'

Caterina eyed Monsieur Pamplemousse curiously as he produced a notebook from under the table. 'It is true, then, that you eat for a living?'

'Don't we all,' said Monsieur Pamplemousse, 'in our different ways?'

'So what will you say about this?'

Monsieur Pamplemousse regarded his plate, then applied his knife to the steak. 'I shall say that the meat is of good quality and that it has been cooked as I asked it to be. It is pink in the middle and juicy – not dried out. The *pommes frites* could be crisper; they have been kept a little too long. The *petits pois*, which might have been disappointing, are surprisingly good. They have the right amount of sweetness. The French beans ... *comme ci, comme ça ...*' He shrugged.

'I also have to ask myself the question: would I feel the same way if we were eating in a restaurant instead of hurtling through the night at over one hundred kilometres an hour?' He was tempted to add 'together with a young and undeniably beautiful girl', but it might have sounded too *gauche*, particularly with others around.

'Normally when I am working I eat by myself so that I am not distracted. Unlike taking a photograph of a distant mountain, where it is possible to add a tree or a shrub to give foreground interest. It is easier to be analytical when you eat alone.'

'I am sorry if I am a distraction. I have never been called "foreground interest" before.' It was said with a smile.

'I forgive you.' Monsieur Pamplemousse broke off to add a few more notes. 'For my taste, there are too many vegetables. They are probably trying to make it look like value for money.

'And you? What do you think?' he asked.

'I think,' said Caterina, 'I think it is all very wonderful. I can't tell you what it feels like to be free.'

Monsieur Pamplemousse gazed at her. What was it the poet Lemierre had once said? 'Even when a bird is walking, we sense that it has wings.' Perhaps it went with being brought up in a convent school. When the door to the outside world was opened the inmates often grasped their new-found freedom with both hands.

'Be careful it does not go to your head.'

'But that is exactly what should happen,' said Caterina. 'It is like champagne. Where else should it go?'

14

Monsieur Pamplemousse could think of a dozen answers, but rather than risk getting into deep water he changed the subject.

'What do you plan to do when you leave school?'

'I shall become a model. I get all the magazines.'

It accounted for the weight of her valise. He wondered where she kept them hidden back at the convent. Under the mattress? It was exceedingly doubtful they would be approved reading.

'It is a hard life,' said Monsieur Pamplemousse. 'For every one who reaches the top of the ladder there are hundreds – thousands – who have to content themselves with clinging to the first few rungs. It is also a comparatively short one. Age has no mercy.'

'That makes it all the more of a challenge,' said Caterina simply. 'For those who do make it, there is a fortune waiting. A top model doing the circuits can easily earn $10,000 a show just for marching down a catwalk. Naomi Campbell started out at fifteen. She walked into the offices of *Elle* and sold herself on the strength of a portfolio of photographs. By the time she was twenty-one she had a million in the bank.'

'At that rate,' said Monsieur Pamplemousse drily, 'by the time you are that age you will be able to retire and open up a *boutique* . . . a chain of *boutiques*. You could have one in Rome, another in Paris, one in London . . . another in New York.'

'Why run a shop when you can be paid more to open one for somebody else?'

Monsieur Pamplemousse gazed at her. She had it all worked out. He also had a feeling she was holding back in some way. It all sounded a little too glib. It wasn't just his imagination – his years in the *Sûreté* had given him a sixth sense in such matters. Her eyes were focused on his, and yet the overall effect was that of a television personality reading someone else's lines from an auto-cue. He couldn't help but wonder why.

'Be careful you do not become like a Dugong.'

Caterina looked at him inquiringly.

'A Dugong,' said Monsieur Pamplemousse, 'is a fish which inhabits the Indian Ocean. It reaches a length of four metres and attains a weight of some 700 kilograms. Leather, ivory and oil are obtained from it, and as if that were not enough, its flesh is considered very edible. In almost all respects you could say it is a very successful fish, consequently it is in great demand. So much so that it has completely disappeared from some areas where it once thrived.'

'I shall be careful,' said Caterina simply.

'And your parents? What do they think?'

The girl pulled a face. 'Papà will go mad. If he had his way he would keep me behind walls for the rest of my life. There would be no choice.'

A clattering of china from somewhere below the table broke into their conversation.

'I know one who enjoyed the meal.' Monsieur Pamplemousse wiped his own plate clean with the last of the bread. He pointed to the tray.

'On a more mundane level, right now you have a choice. There is a carton of yoghurt or there is *clafoutis*. It is a fruit-filled pastry from Limousin – made with black cherries.'

The girl's eyes dwelt longingly on the *clafoutis*. 'May I? Would you mind?'

16

Monsieur Pamplemousse put away his notebook. There wasn't much you could say about a yoghurt that hadn't already been said.

'I know what you are thinking. You are thinking if I am to be a model I shouldn't be eating this. But I am lucky . . . I burn it up. See . . .' Reaching across the table she half rose and struck a pose.

Monsieur Pamplemousse hesitated. 'Would you mind if I took your photograph? It would be nice to look back on.'

'I would like that too.'

'In that case I will fetch my camera.'

Monsieur Pamplemousse began the hazardous journey back to his compartment, battling with the sliding doors as the train swayed from side to side. The conductor was putting the finishing touches to making up his bed when he arrived. It took longer than he had anticipated, and he occupied his time reloading the camera with black and white film.

By the time he got back, the dining-car had begun to fill. Someone else was sitting at the table previously occupied by the man with the dark glasses. He reached his own table at the same time as a party of English. They eyed the empty plates.

'Nobody sitting here.' It was a statement rather than a question. The speaker scarcely waited for an answer before unloading his tray.

Monsieur Pamplemousse made a grimace in Caterina's direction. It had been a wasted journey. Now was not the moment for taking pictures. Conscious once again of eyes watching their progress, he led the way out of the car.

It was the girl's idea to make use of his compartment.

17

Not that Monsieur Pamplemousse wished to blame her in any way, of course. He had been a willing partner; but in retrospect and for the record . . .

Having got the attendant to unlock the door, and seeing that Caterina was waiting expectantly, it seemed like a good idea when she suggested it.

She posed easily and without a trace of embarrassment, throwing her head back as she sat on the bed so that her hair cascaded down over her shoulders like an inky-dark mountain stream. Her lips parted as she undid the top button of her dress. She would be equally at home on a cat-walk or in an Italian rice field. Silvana Mangano in *Bitter Rice*? Sophia Loren in *Black Orchid*? It was wrong to compare. Comparisons were odious. She was her own person.

Focusing on her eyes, Monsieur Pamplemousse stepped back into the corridor trying to frame the picture. As he did so, he glanced round to see if he was being watched. It was not quite what he'd had in mind. He wondered if the girl's reflection could be seen by the couple in the next compartment. Clearly, from the rapt expression on their faces, the answer was *oui*.

As the first flash went off the woman pursed her lips. It struck him that she looked like an outsize version of Madame Grante. Probably, like Madame Grante, she went through life voicing silent disapproval. She nudged her husband as the girl took up another position and Monsieur Pamplemousse fired off a second flash. At least she was getting value for money out of her journey. It probably confirmed her worst suspicions of 'the Continentals'.

Monsieur Pamplemousse took some more pictures and

then came to the end of the reel. 'I will send them to you when they are ready.'

'Papà may not approve.' Caterina thought for a moment and then felt in her handbag. 'I will leave you an address.' She tore a piece of paper from a small pad and wrote on it.

Not to be outdone, Monsieur Pamplemousse reached for his wallet. 'Here is my card. It has my telephone number in case there is a problem. I will get the films processed as quickly as possible – before the end of your holiday.'

'You are very kind.' She stood and suddenly leaned forward. 'Thank you for looking after me so well.'

Monsieur Pamplemousse was totally unprepared for the kiss which followed, still less for its nature. The merest double brushing of lips upon cheek, starting with the right and ending with the left, as in Paris or Lyon, he could have taken in his stride. Intuition coupled with reflexes honed to perfection over the years would have enabled him to cope with regional variations; the Ardèche habit of starting on the left and adding a third, or even the Midi method, where four was the preferred number.

Brillat-Savarin, in his learned and often amusing work, *The Physiology of Taste*, devoted a section to the tongue's place in the natural scheme of things. It was a subject dear to the good doctor's heart. Having waxed lyrical on such matters as the number of papillae on the tongue's surface and the amount of saliva furnished by the inside of the cheeks when the two made contact, he then divided the sensation of taste into *direct*, *complete*, and *reflective*.

Caterina's kiss was both direct and complete, and it was

in reflective mood that Monsieur Pamplemousse hovered in his doorway. Like a schoolboy reeling from his first encounter with the opposite sex, he watched her progress down the corridor.

When she reached her compartment she turned and gave a final wave before disappearing inside. Monsieur Pamplemousse returned it weakly. As he did so he caught sight of the conductor, now safely ensconced in his tiny office at the far end of the coach, a position which enabled him to keep a watchful eye on the comings and goings in his domain. He didn't actually utter the words '*Mamma mia!*', but the look on his face said it all: a total lack of comprehension that a man could spend an evening with such a beautiful girl and yet sleep with a bloodhound. It was, thought Monsieur Pamplemousse, a typical Italian attitude.

Retreating into his own compartment, he closed the door and sat on the bed gazing out into the darkness. It was still warm from where she had sat. Recognising the symptoms, Pommes Frites gave his master a despairing look, followed by a deep sigh. It was the kind of sigh a dog emits when it realises it could be in for a bad night.

Monsieur Pamplemousse ignored the interruption. Had not the learned Brillat-Savarin's researches also brought to light certain other facts concerning tongues? Fish had to make do with a simple moveable bone; birds a membranous cartridge. Pommes Frites was as other four-legged creatures, his tongue lacked the power of circulatory motion. Once Pommes Frites' tongue had been given the go-ahead it went straight to its target, veering neither to the right nor to the left. Food scarcely touched the side of his mouth. Reminders that he should chew every mouthful at least thirty times would have been a waste of breath. Osculation was a pleasure denied him.

Monsieur Pamplemousse closed his eyes. Circulatory motion of a brief but undeniably sensuous and exploratory nature had been apparent in every second of Caterina's kiss.

There was a rustle of linen as Pommes Frites climbed up beside him. He pointedly turned round several times, then fell heavily into a heap in the middle of the bed, forcing his master into a corner.

It was Monsieur Pamplemousse's turn to sigh. Having expressed his feelings in no uncertain manner, he went out into the corridor and beckoned to the conductor.

The man took his time over the paperwork he was engaged in. Then, with an exaggerated gesture, he put down his pen and came to see what was required of him.

'Would it be possible to make up an extra bed?'

There was an intake of breath. 'The *signore's* reservation is for a *singolo*.'

'*Oui*,' said Monsieur Pamplemousse patiently. '*Maintenant* I would like *un doppio*.'

Silence reigned.

'*Per favore?*' He pointed to Pommes Frites. '*Per il cane*. For the dog.'

'*Per il cane?*' The man looked him straight in the eye.

Monsieur Pamplemousse reached for his wallet again.

'*Sì, signore. Pronto.*'

Communication established at long last, Monsieur Pamplemousse watched from the corridor while the operation was carried out swiftly and with practised ease.

'*Il cane* – he will be able to climb the ladder, *signore*?'

'I shall be taking the top bunk,' said Monsieur Pamplemousse.

'*Sì signore*.' As the conductor emerged, Monsieur Pamplemousse slipped him some folded notes.

'*Grazie, signore*.' The exchange didn't pass unnoticed by the couple in the next compartment. Clearly they feared the worst.

It was as he retreated into the compartment that Monsieur Pamplemousse caught sight of his reflection in the mirror over the cupboard and noticed the lipstick. He pulled down the blind, slowly undressed, then climbed the ladder to the top bunk.

Tired though he was, sleep eluded him for a while. He had to admit to himself that he found the thought of the girl preparing for bed in her compartment further down the coach strangely disturbing.

He started going over the encounter in his mind, trying to recapture the moment. Caterina's lips, full and inviting, had felt but a foretaste of what lay within and beyond. The experience had been at one and the same time both innocent and yet intensely pleasurable; investigative and exploratory, as natural and unforced as a rosebud bursting forth in spring. He wondered if everyone received the same treatment. Probably. It would be flattering his own ego to think otherwise.

The next thing Monsieur Pamplemousse knew it was morning. He looked at his watch. It showed seven-forty. Hearing the sound of the train changing pitch, he peered round the side of the blind and saw they were passing through Dijon. They must have stopped somewhere during the night, for they were now travelling in the opposite direction.

There was a clear blue sky overhead and the hilly countryside beyond the city was white with frost. Mistletoe grew in profusion on avenues of leafless trees. There was no sign of life anywhere; no people, no animals.

He washed and dressed quickly, swaying with the motion of the train as it gathered speed. It felt as though they were making up for lost time.

Breakfast arrived promptly at eight o'clock on a plastic compartmentalised tray. While the conductor folded up the bunks and restored things to normal, Monsieur Pamplemousse led Pommes Frites outside. He was just in time to see the man he had silently crossed swords with in the dining car the night before disappear along the corridor towards the front of the train. Il Blobbo, as he'd mentally christened him!

The couple next door were exactly as he had last seen them. He wondered idly if they had been sitting up all night. Perhaps the woman was too large for her bunk, or perhaps they had read about the spate of robberies that were reported to have been taking place on sleeper trains from Italy and weren't taking any chances.

Back in his compartment, Monsieur Pamplemousse settled down and began analysing the breakfast. The chief wasn't going to get away with things that easily. A lengthy report wouldn't come amiss.

Espresso coffee in a china cup. Two small packets of *sucre*. Tinned *jus d'ananas*. Bel Paese cheese. A packet containing two thin slices of Dr Jaus *Roggenvollkornbrot* bread – the exact composition of which was translated into Italian, French, English and Spanish. It sounded unappealing in all five languages, but turned out to have a pleasant taste all its own. It went well with the cheese. A bread roll, also done up in plastic. A small pack of butter. A honey-flavoured confection made of naturally leavened cake shaped like a ringed donut. It was called *La ciambellina* and it was both warm and delicious. A packet of *Pan Brace San Carlo* toast. A hygienically wrapped plastic knife and spoon.

Busy with his own thoughts, Pommes Frites crunched noisily at the toast while his master wrote.

Soon after nine-thirty the attendant returned with his passport. Monsieur Pamplemousse was tempted to call on the girl, but decided he would give her a little longer. She would come to him if she needed anything. He wondered how she would be dressed. The demure convent girl or the woman of the world ready to take Paris in her stride? Perhaps she would surprise him once again and appear in something totally different.

He would know soon enough. All the same, on his way back from the toilet at the end of the coach, he couldn't resist knocking on her door.

'It is nearly time.'

He thought he detected an answering call, but there was a sudden upsurge of noise as they roared through a station – it looked like Melun – and he couldn't be certain.

Thirty minutes later, when there was still no sign of the girl, Monsieur Pamplemousse decided to try again. Signalling Pommes Frites to stand guard over their belongings, he went out into the corridor. But he had left it too late. The train was slowing down for its final approach into the Gare de Lyon and he found his way blocked by the Americans: the woman overseeing her husband, who was struggling with a positive mountain of luggage. There was no possible way past, and certainly no hint in the woman's eyes that she might under any circumstances give way before the train had come to a complete stop.

With rather less than his usual good grace, Monsieur Pamplemousse abandoned his attempt to get past. Having collected his belongings, he took his turn in alighting from the train and waited patiently on the *quai* for the girl to appear.

He waited in vain. Patience gradually gave way to mental drumming as one by one the other passengers emerged and still there was no sign of her. It wasn't as though she had a lot of luggage. He tried not to think of the queue for the taxis. Any advantage they might have gained by being in one of the forward coaches was entirely lost.

Sensing Pommes Frites' growing restiveness, Monsieur Pamplemousse glanced round and spotted Il Blobbo again – hovering at the end of the *quai* nearest the main concourse. He was with another man; a look-alike in dress if not in stature. Shorter and fatter, less dapper perhaps, but wearing an equally expensive looking black overcoat and matching fedora hat. As a duo, Monsieur Pamplemousse mentally bracketed them as a pair of high-class undertakers, although since they were both carrying violin cases he assumed they must be musicians.

They appeared to be intercepting some girls who were coming off the train. None of them were any older than Caterina, and since they were wearing red hats similar to the one she had arrived in, he assumed they must be from the same school. One or two stopped to hold a brief conversation, but most shook their heads and hurried on their way.

As the two men saw him looking in their direction they turned and moved off, melting into the already thinning crowd heading towards the exit.

'*Il signore* has forgotten something?'

The conductor held out an arm, barring Monsieur Pamplemousse's progress as the last of the passengers disembarked and he made to climb back on board.

'Not forgotten . . . left. The *signorina*.'

'The *signorina*?' The man looked at him blankly. 'But the *signorina* has already gone. She left as soon as we arrived.'

He waved his clip-board vaguely in the air. 'She went further along the train . . . she wished to be near the door . . . she was in a hurry. *Molto presto! Molto presto!*'

2

MURDER MOST FOUL

The view as they crossed the Seine by the Pont d'Austerlitz did nothing to raise Monsieur Pamplemousse's spirits. Paris was noticeably colder than Rome. The temperature must have dropped several degrees while they had been away. The water, dark and metallic under the leaden sky, looked deceptively calm; a heavily laden barge travelling upstream was having to fight its way against the current. A moth-eaten spaniel occupying the front passenger seat of the taxi, eyed Pommes Frites dispassionately in the rear-view mirror. It received a blank stare in return.

As their driver turned right and accelerated along the Quai Saint Bernard, Monsieur Pamplemousse found himself automatically glancing into other taxis, wondering if he might catch sight of the girl. It was a forlorn hope, but she could have been delayed for some reason.

He felt aggrieved. Aggrieved and somehow let down. Flat was the word. He tried to tell himself that there was no reason in the world why she should have waited for him. Nothing except common courtesy; a commodity which seemed to be getting rarer and rarer in this day and age. It wasn't that he expected any thanks for his trouble, and admittedly he hadn't said he would be escorting her beyond the Gare de Lyon once they reached Paris. The girl wasn't a mind reader; she had no reason to know he was going into the office anyway to collect his car. But she might at least have had the decency to say *adieu*. A wave would have been better than nothing. A kiss blown from the end of the *quai*: something to file away in his memory.

So much for the brief flirtation of the night before. It would teach him not to romanticise. There was no fool like an old fool.

On reflection, Monsieur Pamplemousse was in no particular hurry to get to the office. The last thing he wanted to do was arrive ahead of her and perhaps bump into the Director waiting on the steps. In the circumstances, it would be an embarrassment. But as always when speed was not of the essence, the lights were green all the way and they reached the Esplanade des Invalides in record time.

The vast area was unusually devoid of tourists. The few people abroad had their hands in their pockets, coat collars turned up. The boules players had not yet put in an appearance.

Monsieur Pamplemousse stopped the driver in the rue Fabert, a little short of their destination, ostensibly in order to let Pommes Frites out for a walk. In truth, he wanted to get rid of his *valise* before putting in an appearance at the office. He wasn't in the mood to answer a barrage of questions. A quick in-and-out was the order of the day.

After his long journey, Pommes Frites looked perfectly content to be left to his own devices while his master disappeared into the depths of the underground car park bearing their luggage.

He was still waiting patiently by the same bench ten minutes later when Monsieur Pamplemousse returned, having deposited his films in the art department for Trigaux to process.

By eleven-twenty they were on their way, and shortly before midday Monsieur Pamplemousse was unlocking the door to his apartment in rue Girardon.

As he opened it he could hear the phone ringing, but by the time he had removed his overcoat it had stopped. Pommes Frites made his way into the kitchen and glanced hopefully at his food bowl, but clearly there was no-one at home. The sound of lapping water filled the air.

Monsieur Pamplemousse was about to open the French windows to let in some air when he spied a note propped against a bowl of flowers in the centre of the dining-room table.

It was from Doucette saying she had gone to Melun for the day to see her sister Agathe, who was feeling poorly again. Without either of them realising it, they had probably passed each other that morning travelling in opposite directions. Doucette would have taken the local train from the Gare de Lyon. There was a picnic lunch in the refrigerator. The salad dressing was in a jar on the top shelf. There was also some fresh cheese and some strawberry *barquettes*. Agathe said she had a lot to tell her so she might be late back.

Monsieur Pamplemousse absorbed the news with

mixed feelings. He was beginning to feel hard done by, as though the world had suddenly turned against him. It would have been nice to have been greeted by something other than a note about a cold collation; the smell of a stew simmering on the stove, perhaps, or a *coq au vin* in the making. Even the pungent whiff of some freshly brewed *café* would have been better than nothing. He had even brought back some fresh truffles from Italy; not the white variety from Piedmont, which Doucette didn't really consider proper, but ironically some imported black ones from France, large, succulent and earthy, each separately wrapped in tissue and packed in an airtight plastic container. They would keep, but not for very long.

On the other hand, matters could have been worse. It was Friday; the day when Agathe was wont to cook *tripe à la mode de Caen*, under the mistaken belief that all you had to do was line a casserole with onions and carrots, shove in a kilogram or so of tripe, along with a calf's foot and the rest of the ingredients, leave it all to simmer for about ten hours and something magical would happen. It never did; not when he was there anyway. More often than not something went wrong. Either Agathe didn't add enough water, or else she didn't seal the pastry top completely tight. Once she even forgot to turn the oven on.

Going into the kitchen, Monsieur Pamplemousse encountered Pommes Frites coming out. An empty bowl pushed to the centre of the floor made clear his feelings.

A walk was indicated. A walk as far as the Place de Clichy. Pommes Frites could work up an appetite chasing a few stray cats in the Cimetière de Montmartre and afterwards they would indulge themselves with a leisurely lunch at, say, Le Maquis in the rue Caulaincourt.

Pommes Frites registered approval as his master picked up the telephone and booked a table. It was a sign that things were returning to normal. Basic decisions were being made.

Some three and a half hours were to pass before they returned home, tired but happy.

Monsieur Pamplemousse took off his shoes and lay back on the bed. What was the word he had used in *Le Guide* to categorise the food in the restaurant? *Copieuse*? He saw no reason to recommend a change in his next report. And *cuisine bourgeoise* was the only way to describe a meal which began with *feuilleté au roquefort* – the mountain of cheese still bubbling away in its casing of flaky pastry – followed by *gigot d'agneau rôti* with *pommes Lyonnaise*; the portions of leg of lamb so generous there was scarcely room left on his plate for the potatoes (on reflection, that had been an error of judgement on his part – following cheese in pastry with cheese in potatoes). Sadly, he had been forced to refuse the *plâteau de fromage* in order to leave room for the *tarte sablée aux framboises*.

He closed his eyes in order to contemplate it the better. Pommes Frites' snores from the foot of the bed said it all. If Stock Pots were *Le Guide*'s symbol of excellence, snores were Pommes Frites'. So, too, in a matter of moments were those of his master.

Monsieur Pamplemousse woke to the sound of the phone ringing. He looked at his watch and saw to his horror that it registered seventeen-fifteen. It was not possible. It could not be.

It was not only possible. It was, according to the

Director's secretary, a matter of some urgency.

Monsieur Pamplemousse tried to focus his attention on what she was saying. Having a whole bottle of Côtes-du-Rhône-Villages to himself had been a mistake. His head was throbbing.

'Monsieur Pamplemousse . . . it is Véronique. Forgive my troubling you. I know you must be tired after your journey . . . but I wonder if you can possibly help?'

'I tried several times to get you. *Monsieur le Directeur* wishes to know what the problem is . . .'

'Problem? What problem?' Monsieur Pamplemousse tried to concentrate on what was being said.

'*Monsieur le Directeur* is reluctant to telephone Rome for fear of causing unnecessary alarm, but he wondered if perhaps there was a mix-up at the other end . . .'

'A mix-up?' Monsieur Pamplemousse forced himself into a sitting position. 'Are you saying his *petite cousine* is not with you?'

'*Monsieur le Directeur* waited on the steps for over an hour this morning. When she didn't appear we tried telephoning you, but there was no reply so we thought perhaps the train had been delayed. It was only when we found out that it had arrived on time that we began to get worried.'

'May I speak with the Director himself?' Monsieur Pamplemousse was suddenly wide awake, all his senses working overtime.

'I am afraid that is not possible, Monsieur Pample-mousse. He is with Sister. He fears he may have caught a chill. It is very cold for this time of year and Rambaud had the main doors open . . .'

'Then tell him I will phone as soon as possible.'

'I will see if I can put you through . . .'

'*Non*. I am going out now.'

'But, Monsieur Pamplemousse . . .'

'*A tout à l'heure*, Véronique. Thank you for calling.'

'Monsieur Pamplemousse . . .' Véronique sounded worried.

'What is it?'

'*Monsieur le Directeur* would not wish for any publicity. Only as a last resort, you understand?'

'*Oui*, Véronique. *Je comprends*.'

Monsieur Pamplemousse replaced the receiver with rather more force than he had intended. He understood only too well. Véronique was only doing as she was told, but it was typical of the Director that in a moment of crisis his first thought should be one of fear at being on the receiving end of any kind of adverse publicity. If ever there was a case for telephoning around, this was it. Well, they would have to see. First things first.

He hurried into the bathroom in order to freshen up with some cold water and in a matter of minutes, with Pommes Frites sitting beside him, he was at the wheel of his 2CV heading down the boulevard Magenta in the general direction of the Gare de Lyon.

As yet, he had no clear idea in his head as to why he was going there, or what he would do when they arrived. It was a matter of instinct – of past experience – going back to square one and starting again; much as an electrical repairman might handle a piece of faulty equipment. Check all external connections to make sure they were correct and move on from there. Tedious and painstaking it might be, but more often than not it was what produced results in the end.

Square one was the Gare de Lyon. It was hard to picture, but for all he knew Caterina might still be waiting there, panic having set in when she found herself lost in a strange city. Despite her outward self-confidence, she was still only a schoolgirl, and a schoolgirl with very little experience of the outside world at that. The *gare*, with its multitude of layers, each one teeming with travellers indifferent to anyone's problems but their own, was about as far removed from the cloistered calm of a convent as it was possible to imagine. She could have met with an accident, or been knocked down and suffered a loss of memory – stranger things had been known. The possibilities were endless. Mugged? Heaven forbid! He would never hear the last of it.

In any event, it would be a start. For the moment he refused to allow thoughts of anything more serious to enter his mind. The explanation, when it came, would probably turn out to be something quite mundane.

It was the height of the evening rush hour and traffic was heavy; the reverse of his morning journey. Every junction had its hold-up. Lorries fighting their way into the city, cars fighting their way out, with no quarter given on either side. Autobuses exerting their priority over other traffic – the drivers with their telephones at the ready in case a total *impasse* was reached.

Finding somewhere to park his *deux chevaux* was yet another problem. It took him something over ten minutes before he found a suitable gap in a side street behind the *gare*. As they made their way towards the entrance the clock in the belfry above the Big Ben bar showed midday on one face, on another four-twenty. The

34

architect, Marius Toudoire, would not have been pleased. Monsieur Pamplemousse looked at his watch. It said eighteen-fifteen.

Inside the station, he set off on a quick voyage of exploration, retracing much the same path he had followed that morning. As before, he soon gave it up as a bad job. There were innumerable places Caterina could still be without having left the building. The Gare de Lyon was vast, and it had grown larger still since its integration with the RER high-speed underground system. It would take for ever to search all the different levels thoroughly, particularly with so many people milling around.

Monsieur Pamplemousse returned to the main concourse serving the *Grandes Lignes* and looked around and up in search of inspiration. It came almost immediately in the shape of the Departures board.

Scanning it for want of something better to do, he registered the fact that the train they had travelled up on – the Palatino – was scheduled to leave for Rome in less than half an hour's time. At eighteen-forty-nine to be precise. *Quai* 'J'. It was not beyond the bounds of possibility that the same staff would be manning it for the return journey. Most of them would be going home.

The train was already in the *quai*. Looking slightly old-fashioned amongst the chic orange and grey livery of the TGVs, it still managed to exude an air of quiet superiority; of the way things *should* be done. Inside the first-class compartments people were unpacking their bags; hanging suits and dresses on to hooks; others had already drawn their blinds. Several coaches along, Monsieur Pamplemousse saw a familiar figure in brown clutching a clip-board.

As they drew near there was a glint of recognition. An official hand reached out for his ticket.

Monsieur Pamplemousse shook his head. 'We are not travelling.' He decided to plunge straight in. For the moment there was a lull. Quite possibly it wouldn't last very long. 'I was wondering if I might ask you a few questions?'

'Questions, *signore*?' There was the faintest change of expression on the conductor's face.

Before it had time to harden, Monsieur Pamplemousse felt for his wallet. It was becoming an expensive operation.

'Last night I travelled up from Rome with a girl . . .'

'*Sì, signore.*' The man's face lit up again. 'I remember her well . . .' He sought for the right words. '*Che bella figura!*'

'It was my intention to escort her to her destination,' said Monsieur Pamplemousse. 'But somehow in the rush we missed each other. You may remember. I looked for her at the front of the *quai*, but . . .'

'But she got off further down the train, *signore*.'

'Further *down* the train?' Monsieur Pamplemousse looked at the man in amazement. 'You mean she didn't go towards the front?'

'She said she was in a hurry and I told her to leave nearer the middle. I explained to her that it is often quicker. There are exits all the way along the *quai*. Also it is often easier for taxis. There is another rank at the back of the *gare*. Everyone makes for the front.'

Monsieur Pamplemousse looked aggrieved. 'Why did you not tell me that when I spoke to you yesterday morning?'

'You did not ask me, *signore*. As I remember it you simply asked me if I had seen her.'

The man hesitated. 'I think she was trying to avoid someone. That is why she wished to leave as quickly as possible.'

Monsieur Pamplemousse pondered the remark. Was it possible that Caterina had not wanted to see him? His pride took a momentary fall.

As though reading his thoughts, the conductor shook his head emphatically. 'No, *signore*. Not you. There was someone else. Another person.' He hesitated as a couple drew near, the woman pushing a trolley laden with luggage, the man comparing the number on their tickets with the one on the carriage. An electric trolley driven by a bearded porter wove its way past them.

Realising he was running out of time and that he was still holding his wallet, Monsieur Pamplemousse made to open it. 'This other person. Was it a man?'

The conductor covered the wallet with his clip-board. 'It is not necessary, *signore*.' He hesitated again, looking over his shoulder as though not wanting to be overheard. 'Come back in a little while. When the rush has died down. We can talk then.'

Accepting the man at his word, Monsieur Pamplemousse was about to set off back down the *quai* towards the main concourse when he spied one of the secondary exits. Acting on an impulse, he made his way down some stairs and found himself in a vast marble concourse on a lower level.

It was true what the conductor had said. Arrowed TAXIS signs pointed beyond the shops towards an exit at the rear of the building. Ambling after his master,

Pommes Frites paused at the top of the stairs and stared back at the train as though some nameless unhappiness had entered his soul.

But he paused in vain, for Monsieur Pamplemousse had his mind on other things. The Director for a start. He made for a row of telephones tucked away in a corner near the foot of the stairs and searched for his *télécarte*. It was time he checked in. For all he knew, Caterina might have turned up by now and he could be wasting his time.

It was a felicitous thought, but one that alas was not to be borne out in fact. The Director's first words set the tone of the conversation. It was worse than Monsieur Pamplemousse had feared. Total disbelief emanated from every nuance of every word.

'Pamplemousse, would you mind repeating your last utterance. I feel I may have misheard you.'

Monsieur Pamplemousse decided to play for time.

'I said, *Monsieur*, that conversation is a little difficult on account of the ambient noise level in the *gare*.' Even as he spoke, he was conscious of the fact that compared with the hustle and bustle of the main concourse, he had actually stumbled on an oasis of relative quiet. He wished now he had stayed put; it would have made matters a little easier.

Catching sight of the lugubrious expression on Pommes Frites' face as he hung on his master's every word, Monsieur Pamplemousse buried himself deeper still into the screened telephone booth, tightening his grip on the receiver as he did so. Pursing his lips, he went into his 'departure of the Orient Express for sunnier climes' routine. It always went down well with his colleagues, although to be truthful he only ever performed it towards the ending of an evening, when everyone else was suitably primed, not to say well oiled. A man at the adjoining telephone stopped talking for a moment in order to listen, then said something into the receiver.

Monsieur Pamplemousse ignored it. Clearly his own audience at the other end of the line was in a less receptive mood. Disenchantment set in almost immediately. Hardly had he completed his interpretation of a *chef de train* blowing a warning blast on his whistle than there was an explosion in his left ear which was little short of being on the threshold of pain.

'Pamplemousse! I have had a particularly trying day. I do not wish to listen to the kind of charade you trot out every year at the staff outing. Furthermore, the last steam train left the Gare de Lyon over forty years ago. Will you please answer my question. Did I or did I not hear you say you have lost Caterina? I trust my ears deceived me.'

Monsieur Pamplemousse took a deep breath. 'I said I couldn't find her, *Monsieur*.'

'That is splitting hairs, Pamplemousse!' barked the Director. 'What have you done with her?'

Ignoring the unfairness of the question, Monsieur Pamplemousse essayed a run-down of his end of the story. There was nothing like setting out the facts in detail to another person to help crystallise one's own thoughts.

'*I* have done nothing with her, *Monsieur*. I took *petit déjeuner* early as I wished to be alone in order to write up my notes so that they would be ready for you at the earliest possible moment. Apropos of which, I may say the catering facilities were not quite as they were described to me. Alas, the days of *le grand wagon salle à manger* are no longer with us. The buffet car is admirable in its way, but one might as well be eating in a Jumbo jet. There is no longer a silver service. The salt and pepper comes in little plastic packets . . .'

'This is dreadful news, Pamplemousse.'

'It is a sign of the times, *Monsieur*.'

'I was referring to *ma petite cousine*, Caterina,' said the Director. 'Did she not join you for *petit déjeuner*?'

'No, *Monsieur*, she did not. We both took breakfast in our respective compartments. It was brought round on a tray by the conductor. When we were getting near Paris I knocked loudly on Caterina's door to warn her. I am almost certain I heard her call out to thank me. That being so, I fully expected to see her ready and waiting as we entered the *gare*, but there was no sign.

'Unfortunately my own departure was delayed for several minutes by an extremely large American lady with a great many *valises*. Even Pommes Frites couldn't get past. I suspect she was being deliberately difficult.

'When I finally managed to alight I was told by the conductor that Caterina had made her way to another coach shortly before I appeared. I assumed he meant nearer the front, but I have just learned I was mistaken. Since when I haven't seen her.'

'I say again, Pamplemousse, this is dreadful news. I charged you with her safe keeping. You have failed to carry out my orders.'

'With respect, *Monsieur*, that is not entirely correct. You merely suggested that as I was investigating the catering facilities on the Palatino and as *by chance* your *petite cousine* happened to be travelling on the same train, we could keep each other company. Caterina is no longer a child, *Monsieur*. Furthermore, I must remind you I am employed by *Le Guide* as an Inspector of hotels and catering establishments, not as a nursemaid. I assume you are not suggesting I should have shared Caterina's sleeping compartment. There is no other way I could have kept my eyes on her all the time. Unless, of course, you wanted me to camp out in the corridor. There are little fold-down seats. I could have sat on one of those all night. Madame Grante would have been pleased. It would have saved *Le Guide* a considerable sum.'

There was a moment's silence before the Director spoke again.

'Forgive me, Aristide. I am overwrought.'

Monsieur Pamplemousse relaxed. The apology sounded genuine enough. The chief always grew a bit edgy towards publication day.

'I must admit to feeling a little put out that she hadn't even waited to say goodbye, *Monsieur*. I put it down to the forgetfulness of the young. Forgetfulness coupled with the excitement of the occasion. I assumed she was making her way straight to your office.'

'What time did the train arrive?'

'Ten-nineteen, *Monsieur*. It was two minutes late. There was a slight air of restiveness everywhere. Watches were being consulted. I have never seen the *gare* so crowded on a Saturday morning. It was a seething mass of schoolchildren going on their skiing holidays. I had to fight my way through. I tried mounting the grand staircase leading to *Le Train Bleu* restaurant, but I encountered a certain amount of resistance. Pommes Frites was dying to obey the call of nature by then and not unnaturally when he saw the Christmas trees he took advantage of them. I became involved in an argument with one of the waiters

41

who was cleaning the stairs and that delayed matters still further . . .'

'Christmas trees?' barked the Director. 'In March?'

'*Exactement, Monsieur*. I trust the whole thing will be removed at the end of the skiing season. It is an eyesore.'

'They used to serve the best dry martini in Paris,' said the Director dreamily. 'The barman merely showed the label on the vermouth bottle to the gin.'

'It is possible, *Monsieur*, that he still does,' said Monsieur Pamplemousse.

Taking advantage of the change in the conversation he tried to maintain the hopeful note he had struck.

'It is the usual syndrome when someone is late, *Monsieur*. First there is irritation. Then one becomes cross. Crossness gives way to worry. Finally, when they do arrive, there is relief; relief mixed with guilt at ever having doubted them. It is early days to get one's *culottes* in a twist. There could be a dozen reasons why Caterina is late. She may have met an old friend, or she may have decided to do some shopping before she came to see you.'

'It is not my *culottes* I am worried about, Pamplemousse,' said the Director meaningly. 'We are talking about the *culottes* of a young girl who has spent much of her life in a convent. We all know what that means.'

'We do, *Monsieur*?'

'It is a highly charged atmosphere, Pamplemousse. Sex is always uppermost in the mind of the pupils. Couple that with a sense of guilt instilled at an early age by the Sisters and you have a sure-fire recipe for trouble. The nearest comparison which springs to mind is that of a piece of dry tinderwood awaiting the striking of the first match.'

'My knowledge of convent life, *Monsieur*, is limited. I

know only those things I have heard at second or even third hand.'

'Me too, Pamplemousse. Me too. But as a boy my imagination was much exercised by a book called *The Dreadful Disclosures of Maria Monk*. It was required "under the desk" reading at the *lycée*.'

'Surely things have changed since that was written, *Monsieur*?'

'I think not, Aristide. I think not. Only in matters of detail. The book is probably part of the National Curriculum now, but I strongly suspect lascivious thoughts are still rife in the minds of those attending such establishments – fed as they are on a diet of fish.'

'We ordered steak for dinner last night, *Monsieur* . . .'

'The damage is done, Pamplemousse,' said the Director impatiently, 'It is a well-known fact that those whose diet consists largely of fish procreate like the proverbial *lapins*. It is the presence of so much phosphorus. Take any fishing community in the world. Notwithstanding the fact that many of the men-folk are away for long periods of time, the birth-rate is invariably above the national average. That is why I fear your comment on twisted *culottes* was singularly misplaced.'

Monsieur Pamplemousse remained silent for a moment or two. He was beginning to wish he had never used the phrase. The Director was fond of throwing in statements one longed to disprove. Apart from which, it was hardly the time to let fall the fact that the last time he had seen Caterina he doubted if her *culottes* were of a type to have passed muster at her convent's weekly knicker inspection, let alone have sufficient material in their construction to allow for much in the way of twisting.

He looked at his watch. It showed eighteen-thirty-five. 'If you will forgive me, *Monsieur*, I must go. I have been questioning the conductor of the Palatino. He may have some vital information.'

Even as he spoke, Monsieur Pamplemousse realised he hadn't the slightest idea what Caterina had been wearing. Her school outfit or something a little more chic?

'If I draw a blank I will telephone the police. Although I doubt if they will do very much at this stage other than circulate a description.'

There was a sharp intake of breath at the other end of the line. 'That is the very last thing you must do, Pamplemousse.'

'But, *Monsieur* . . .'

'No *buts*, Pamplemousse. I cannot explain matters over the telephone – there are certain complications. Continue your present inquiries by all means, but I suggest that as soon as they are complete you return to Headquarters, *tout de suite*. I will await your arrival.'

'But, *Monsieur* . . .'

'*Immédiatement!*'

Monsieur Pamplemousse replaced the receiver and removed his *télécarte*.

Quite understandably, the chief had sounded worried. But there had been something else as well: overtones of some deeper emotion; for want of a better word, a distinct note of apprehension – apprehension bordering on panic.

Monsieur Pamplemousse's own fears, which until that moment had lain dormant, perhaps if he was completely honest with himself, had been deliberately swept under the carpet, now surfaced. His pace quickened as he led the way back up the stairs.

As though infected by the same sense of urgency, Pommes Frites ran on ahead and was waiting by the Palatino as his master emerged from the stairway.

Monsieur Pamplemousse looked for the conductor, but he was nowhere to be seen. Assuming the man was inside the coach making last-minute preparations for the train's departure, he made his way along the *quai* peering in through the windows. But he drew a blank. Unfamiliar faces stared back at him, as though resenting the intrusion of a peeping tom. It was vexing to say the least.

With a feeling of impatience he boarded the train and looked inside the little office at the end of the coach. It was empty. There was a clip-board and a small pile of ticket stubs on the table. Alongside it was a tray with some bottles of mineral water, several glasses and an opener.

He checked the nearby toilet and once again drew a blank. A passenger standing in the corridor waving a last goodbye to someone outside eyed him curiously.

'*Le chef de train*,' said Monsieur Pamplemousse. 'The conductor. I was looking for him.'

The man gave a shrug. 'I'm sorry. I don't know. He was here earlier.' He resumed his waving, more urgently this time.

Monsieur Pamplemousse looked at his watch. It was time he left. It would be the final straw if he found himself trapped on board. Dijon was probably the first stop.

Calling Pommes Frites to follow, he made a less than dignified exit on to the *quai*. They were only just in time. The two-minute warning of the train's imminent departure was already being made over the loudspeakers. First in French, then in English, then in Italian.

Those on the *quai* who had come to see their nearest and dearest safely on their way stood back a little as the hands on the clock above the stairs moved inexorably closer to departure time. There was the faintest jolt from the Palatino as it prepared to leave. Somewhere towards the front came the sound of a whistle being blown and moments later, as the second hand reached the vertical, the train began to move.

Impatience gave way to frustration and a sense of failure as Monsieur Pamplemousse watched the coaches glide past, gradually gathering speed. The engine that had brought the train into the *quai* followed on at a respectful distance, perhaps some twenty or thirty metres or so behind, the driver clearly anxious to return to his depot.

As it went past Monsieur Pamplemousse turned and began walking slowly back up the *quai* towards the main concourse. It was infuriating. The conductor must have been deliberately avoiding him. There was no other explanation. And for what reason? Perhaps they should have stayed on board after all until the man put in an appearance.

He was so engrossed in his thoughts he was totally unaware of what was going on around him.

At last, sensing that for some reason best known to himself, Pommes Frites was trying to attract his attention, he glanced up impatiently and was just in time to see a shadowy figure in a dark overcoat ducking beneath a gap between two coaches of a stationary train waiting alongside the adjoining *quai*.

Even from the back, there was something familiar about the person, but before he had time to call out, that train, too, began to move. It gave him quite a turn, for he

46

felt sure the man must have been caught by it before he had a chance to scramble clear.

Monsieur Pamplemousse stood rooted to the spot for a moment, half expecting to see the worst as the last of the carriages went past, but instead all that remained was an almost empty *quai*. Whoever it was must have escaped by the skin of his teeth and made a bolt for it.

Gradually he became aware of yet another distraction; voices coming from further up his own *quai*, near to where he had been standing only minutes before.

Turning round, he saw that the engine which had brought the Palatino into the *gare* had ground to a halt alongside a small group of officials. He recognised the bearded porter among them. They were staring down at something on the line.

With a growing sense of foreboding, Monsieur Pamplemousse made his way back up the *quai*. As he drew near the group he followed the direction of their gaze and saw a figure in brown sitting in the gap between the two tracks. It was the conductor from the Palatino.

He looked for all the world as though he were taking part in a game of cards. From the total lack of expression in the eyes he could have been playing a hand of poker. Only the decorated head of a silver hat pin protruding from his right ear and a small trickle of blood running down behind his collar proclaimed the truth. The pointed end of the pin must have entered his brain. Death would have been both instantaneous and soundless.

Alongside the man lay a pair of dark glasses, one lens of which was smashed as though it had been trampled underfoot.

Monsieur Pamplemousse gazed at the motionless

figure for several seconds, trying to absorb the fact and the meaning behind it, before he turned and began retracing his steps along the *quai*, slowly at first, then with gathering speed.

Mindful of the Director's warning, and conscious that others were watching his movements, he called Pommes Frites to heel as they drew level with an exit and as though obeying a sudden whim, stopped abruptly and led the way quickly down the steps, feeling for his car keys as he went.

Reaching the lower level rather quicker than he had on the previous occasion, Monsieur Pamplemousse threw dignity to the wind and broke into a run. There were times when discretion was the better part of valour, and this was undoubtedly one of them.

3

OUT ON A LIMB

Le Guide's headquarters was ablaze with light. Everyone was working late. It was the busy time of the year.

Rambaud – who rarely emerged from his gate-keeper's office when there was an 'r' in the month – had stationed himself outside the main entrance. He wore a scarf round his neck to keep warm. The large wooden doors, as discreet in their way as the entrance to a London club, unadorned by anything so plebeian as a nameplate and normally kept closed to the outside world, were wide open. When he caught sight of Monsieur Pamplemousse's car approaching Rambaud stood to one side and signalled him to enter. It was an unheard of occurrence. Normally parking space in the inner courtyard was for VIPs only, the sole exception being a carefully marked area set aside for *Monsieur le Directeur* near the entrance to his private elevator.

One of the girls in reception was waiting for them by the lift. Rambaud must have given prior warning of their arrival, for she was holding the door open in readiness.

'*Merci.*'

As Monsieur Pamplemousse entered the lift the girl handed him, a large, official-looking brown envelope. It bore the Art Department's emblem. If Trigaux had done his stuff with the films it might well come in useful.

They were whisked up to the seventh floor without stopping once. As the doors slid open he saw Véronique, the Director's secretary, standing outside. She led the way along the thickly carpeted corridor.

'How was Rome?'

'Warmer than here,' said Monsieur Pamplemousse. 'The children were mostly in costume. They were throwing confetti everywhere. It was the last big festival before Lent.'

'And the food? Did you eat well?' Clearly the subject of the Director's *cousine* was not up for discussion.

'On the first evening I had *culatello di zibello*. It is a *prosciutto* made from a knuckle of ham which has been aged, then soaked in sparkling red Lambrusco. It was possibly the most beautiful ham I have ever tasted; so soft it almost melted in the mouth. I followed that with *tortellini alla panna*. It was a speciality of the house and it was served covered with thinly sliced truffles. The taste comes back to me every time I think of it.'

He followed Véronique into her outer office and waited while she pressed a buzzer.

'Yesterday for *déjeuner* I ordered baked baby lamb with rosemary. It was accompanied by a green salad and it was so good Pommes Frites had a second helping. He made short work of the bones as well.'

Véronique opened her desk drawer and took out an imaginary violin which she began to play.

'Work, work, all the time work. It must be unbearably hard at times.'

Monsieur Pamplemousse put on his injured look. 'On both occasions the wine was of the most ordinary. The house *vino rosso*, which came in a glass jug. The information may come in useful if we ever do an Italian edition of *Le Guide*.'

Véronique stopped playing. 'Pigs might fly.' She tried buzzing the Director again. There was still no response.

'I should go on in. And watch out – I think *Monsieur le Directeur* is in one of his moods.'

Unexpectedly, despite the cold, the Director was standing outside on his balcony gazing into space. He looked in sober mood as he turned to greet his subordinate.

'Aristide, you are the last person in the world I would have wished this to happen to.' He gave a shiver as he came back into his office, closing the French windows behind him.

'But, *Monsieur*, it is I who should feel badly about the whole thing. Even now it is hard to say how it came about.'

Avoiding Monsieur Pamplemousse's gaze, the Director motioned him to sit, then crossed to the far side of the room. He looked as though he had aged ten years.

'Let me get you a drink.'

Catching sight of the portrait of Monsieur Hippolyte Duval, founder of *Le Guide*, it struck Monsieur Pamplemousse that for once he, too, seemed to be avoiding his gaze. Normally, those magnetic ice-blue eyes, captured in oils by the artist at the turn of the century, followed visitors everywhere they went in the room; there was no escaping them. Now, they seemed to be gazing into the middle distance. It must have been an optical illusion for as soon as the Director opened the door to his drinks cupboard and the light came on the feeling disappeared.

'A little white wine, *Monsieur*. A glass of Muscadet, perhaps?' He suddenly realised how thirsty he felt.

'Why not have something stronger?' The Director reached for a bottle of cognac. 'A glass of my Roullet *Très Rare Hors d'Age – numero vingt-six*, perhaps? Everyone should have at least one glass before they die.'

Monsieur Pamplemousse pretended not to have noticed the last remark. Véronique was right. The chief was in a downcast mood and no mistake. Stifling any kind of response, he watched while a more than generous measure was poured. Clearly something was afoot. Even Pommes Frites shifted uneasily as he recognised the signs.

Putting a brave face on matters, Monsieur Pamplemousse tried to turn the conversation in a happier direction.

'Should you ever choose to embark on an Italian edition of *Le Guide*, *Monsieur*, you may like to know that we had an excellent *dîner* in Rome the night before last. It was in a little family restaurant called Colline Emiliane, not far from the Piazza Barbarini . . .'

'I doubt, Pamplemousse, if any of us will be venturing on to Italian soil for some time to come,' said the Director gloomily.

He held out a large, balloon-shaped glass. Monsieur Pamplemousse took it reverently with both hands, warming the contents before lifting it to his nose. He was rewarded by a superbly rich and opulent bouquet.

'Perhaps,' said the Director, seating himself behind his

desk, 'I should begin at the beginning.'

'It is always a good place to start, *Monsieur*.'

'The name Caterina, Pamplemousse, is derived from a Greek word meaning pure. I don't know what impressions you may have formed, but I think you must agree that if ever the choice of a name was inappropriate it has to be that with which Chantal's *petite cousine* was christened.'

Even if Monsieur Pamplemousse had been inclined to answer, he wasn't given the chance.

'She has always led a sheltered existence,' continued the Director. 'Her formative years were spent on her parents' estate. She was never allowed outside its four walls. They have always guarded her chastity. She is an only daughter, her mother's pride and joy, the *pomme* of Uncle Rocco's *oeil*, and when she began to show unmistakable signs of maturity she was dispatched to a convent for safe keeping.

'As things turned out it was a disastrous move. Desires held in check all those years blossomed as they emerged from beneath the metaphorical bed-clothes. Loins which hitherto had only been exercised in the picking of orange blossom, were girded before being unleashed on an ill-prepared world. It must have been somewhat akin to Mount Vesuvius erupting after a particularly hot summer. Imagine her parents' distress when, after only a week in her new surroundings, she was asked to leave.'

'All young girls are high-spirited, *Monsieur*. Perhaps she found the regime too strict. Was it a Jesuit establishment?'

'This was not a simple case of high spirits, Pamplemousse. She pushed the Mother Superior into the swimming pool. Having been caught behind the changing rooms in *flagrante delicto* with a young gardener, she was trying to make good her escape when she was intercepted. Unfortunately the encounter took place near the deep end of the pool, and as swimming had not been part of the curriculum when the Mother Superior was a child it nearly ended in disaster. Nuns' garments weigh exceedingly heavy when they are steeped in water.'

'Is that so, *Monsieur*?'

The Director chose to ignore the interruption. 'Caterina was judged to be a corrupting influence on the other girls in her class,' he continued. 'She was told to pack her belongings and her parents were sent for. But Uncle Rocco, who has connections with the Vatican, persuaded the powers that be to change their minds. As a result they now have one of the finest tennis courts that money can buy.'

'And the gardener, *Monsieur*? What happened to him?'

The Director shrugged. 'He was never seen again. But that was no problem. I am told that even though they pay only the minimum rates there is always a sizeable queue of applicants for the post. But that is a thing of the past. The nuns have learned their lesson and they are paying the price with backs bent over the hoe.'

'But with respect, *Monsieur*, we are living in the latter half of the twentieth century . . .'

'Correction, Pamplemousse. *We* may be living in the latter half of the twentieth century, but not everyone recognises that fact, still less do they allow others to enjoy the benefits that go with it. Some people – particularly those who are used to living in a relatively closed community – set great store by what they consider to be their "property". They guard it assiduously. That is the case with Uncle Rocco and his daughter and that is why I entrusted you with the mission.

'Anticipating her safe arrival, our own gardeners have been briefed. Warnings have been issued. The pool has been drained. And now...'

'I wish you had told me all this earlier, *Monsieur*. To be forewarned is to be forearmed.'

'You are not the only one, Pamplemousse. You are not the only one. My wife and I discussed the matter at great length and in the end Chantal felt the least said the better. We did not wish to worry you unduly.'

Monsieur Pamplemousse sipped his brandy thoughtfully. 'I still do not understand, *Monsieur*, why you are so against calling in the police. Surely, a discreet word in the right quarters...'

'That is out of the question, Pamplemousse. Utterly out of the question. Uncle Rocco is impatient with authority. In his eyes there are no "right" quarters. He is a law unto himself. We shall need to mobilise our own forces – and quickly. Speed is of the essence. He will be awaiting a call to hear that all is well and there is a limit to the number of excuses I can find when he asks to speak to his daughter. The sound of a departing steam train, however well executed, will cut little ice in the circumstances.'

'But, surely, *Monsieur*...'

'There is no "surely" about it, Pamplemousse. Chantal's Uncle Rocco is a very powerful person and Chantal is his favourite niece. He is also by nature the sort of person who at the slightest whim would pick up a telephone and erase her from his memory with no more thought than he would put to telling the captain of one of his merchant ships to alter course for the Azores. He is also, I may say, perfectly capable of erasing others from his memory too.'

And from his will, thought Monsieur Pamplemousse. That had to be it: the reason for his boss's unhappiness. The more some people had, the more they wanted.

'Life will not be worth living once he gets to hear what has occurred,' said the Director.

'But what can he do, *Monsieur*? He may be powerful in the world of shipping, and I agree that he has good reason to be upset . . . but here in Paris . . .'

The Director dithered for a moment or two, making a show of tidying his desk before replying. 'Uncle Rocco's interests are not entirely confined to maritime matters, Pamplemousse,' he said at last. 'He is involved in many things. He has his fingers in a multitude of pies. Buying and selling . . . the construction business . . . his tentacles are like those of an octopus and they stretch far beyond the confines of the island where he lives. He has connections everywhere.'

'He lives on an island, *Monsieur*?' The word 'tentacles' coupled with that of 'island' caused faint warning bells to start sounding in the back of Monsieur Pamplemousse's head. 'I assumed he lived somewhere near Rome.'

'Did I say that?' asked the Director innocently.

'No, *Monsieur*, you did not. I merely assumed . . .'

Draining his glass, the Director rose and crossed to the French windows, where he stood gazing out across Paris. The golden dome of St Louis des Invalides gleamed dully in the cloud-filtered sunset. Much further away and to its left, the equally distinctive dome of the Sacré Coeur on the heights of Montmartre seemed nearer than usual; a hint, perhaps, that rain was on the way.

But Monsieur Pamplemousse noticed none of these things. His thoughts were concentrated on more immediate matters. The Director's behaviour for a start; his wife Chantal's unexpected absence – they all began to add up. He had a sudden mental picture of the conductor's body sitting where it had been placed on the railway track. At the time the method of killing had seemed extraordinarily bizarre, now he wasn't so sure.

'What was the name of the island where Caterina spent her childhood, *Monsieur*?'

The Director waved one hand vaguely in a westerly direction. 'Corsica, Sardinia ... there are so many ... I really cannot remember which one.'

'Were you to be gifted with extraordinarily long sight,' persisted Monsieur Pamplemousse, 'could you, from where you are standing, *Monsieur*, perhaps see beyond Corsica, and beyond Sardinia, to an island known as Sicily?'

'Sicily!' There was barely a split second's hesitation, but it was more than sufficient. 'That was it. Thank you, Pamplemousse. It all comes back to me now. An interesting island, steeped in history. First colonised by man towards the end of the Ice Age. Occupied for a time, according to Greek mythology, by a race of one-eyed cyclopean giants of cannibalistic propensities. There was also the Barbarian period; the Byzantine period; the Arab period ...'

'The Cosa Nostra period?' broke in Monsieur Pamplemousse. 'Which began shortly after Garibaldi drove out the last of the Bourbon kings and which has been active ever since.'

'Sicily has always been a turbulent isle,' said the Director evasively, turning his back on the outside world. 'Greeks, Romans, Barbarians, the Emperors of Byzantium, the Arabs, the Normans and the Germans; they have all occupied it at various times.

'Over the centuries the inhabitants have had more than their fair share of troubles, and it is perhaps not surprising that they have turned to those who are prepared to help. Two thousand years of foreign occupation and despotic rule have also taught them to keep their mouths shut. I need hardly remind you, Aristide, that "Cosa Nostra" means "our affair".'

The Director raised his hand as he saw Monsieur Pamplemousse was about to interject.

'Please don't misunderstand me. I am not for one moment saying the Mafia is a force for good – quite the reverse. Their motivation is simply one of greed. Where there is easy money to be made, that is where you will find them. They rule by fear and once you are a member there is only one way out – feet first.

'Having said that, there have been times when the State has been undeniably bad; hopelessly out of touch with the needs of its people and seemingly indifferent to their fate. There are those – mostly poor peasants, who in times past have felt abandoned by their government – who might say that life would be infinitely less happy and secure without the protection of the Uncle Caputos of this world. I would not like to sit in judgement of that belief. There, but for the Grace of God, Aristide, go I.'

'Caputo?' Monsieur Pamplemousse gave a start. 'But, did you not say, *Monsieur*, that the name of your wife's uncle is Rocco?'

The Director brushed aside the remark. 'It is merely a nickname. A childish appellation Chantal bestowed on him when she was small. Her Uncle Rocco is not, I fear, a very good loser. Sometimes, when they were playing together and he found things weren't going his way he would bring the game to an abrupt end – either by sending her off to play hide and seek and then never going after her, or else by pretending to shoot her, saying "Right, Chantal, your time is up – you are *caputo*." She has never forgotten the fact. Over the years it became something of a joke in the family.'

Monsieur Pamplemousse digested the information slowly and carefully.

'And when he is not playing games, *Monsieur*, what does Uncle Caputo do then?'

'This and that,' said the Director vaguely. 'I understand he plays a prominent role in the Sicilian laundry business. He is highly thought of in ecclesiastical circles.'

'You mean – he takes in the Vatican's washing?'

The Director glared at Monsieur Pamplemousse. 'You know perfectly well what I mean, Pamplemousse. Chantal's Uncle Caputo happens to enjoy a good relationship with a certain dignitary in the church, an official holding high office whose duties take him to the mainland from time to time. This person is not averse to lining his cassock with whatever he is given, in return for enjoying the many benefits concomitant with travelling first class, not the least of which is that of having extra space

59

between the seats. It is a happy arrangement on both sides.'

'Would it be true to say, *Monsieur*, that within your own family circle Il Signor Rocco is more of a Godfather than an uncle?'

The Director gazed unhappily at Monsieur Pamplemousse. 'If you insist on my spelling it out, Pamplemousse, I am saying that Chantal's Uncle Rocco is an important member of the Cosa Nostra and as such he commands respect. People cross swords with him at their peril. He does not live in an unnumbered house in an unnamed street on the island of Sicily for nothing.'

'In what other directions do Uncle Rocco's tentacles travel, *Monsieur*?'

'He was very much into cigarettes at one time. A container-load is worth a great deal and is easily disposed of – especially if you happen to control all the machines which dispense them. Currently, I understand he is very much interested in caviar. It is a matter of bartering. The Russian Mafia, such as it is, will do anything for foreign currency. I am told that if you hail a taxi in Moscow the first question the driver asks is not where are you going, but how you wish to pay? If you say roubles, then he goes on his way leaving you stranded.

'Forty francs' worth of Beluga caviare at source is worth the equivalent of 20,000 francs in Rome and corruption abounds.

'Kidnapping, protection, extortion, loan sharking . . . all the usual things. All, that is, except gambling and prostitution. It is against the principles of the Sicilian Cosa Nostra to be involved in either – they leave that to their American counterparts. Gambling indicates a weakness which they have no wish to exploit lest they themselves get tainted in the process, and for a Sicilian, living on a woman's earnings is dishonourable.

'As a man of honour, that is one of the principal reasons why Uncle Caputo is so protective of his only daughter. To date he has always kept her free from the gaze of other men. Letting her come to stay in Paris only came about as a result of much pleading on her part and an undertaking on ours that we would never let her out of our sight. On pain, Pamplemousse, of certain anatomical modifications to our persons as yet hardly touched on by the medical *journaux* should we fail in our task.'

'If that is the case, *Monsieur*, why did you agree to have her to stay?'

'Why do you pay your income tax, Aristide? Certainly not because you do not wish to hurt the feelings of those in power by declining.'

'Would it not have been better to have gone to Rome yourself?'

The Director raised his hands. 'Work, Aristide, work! It never goes away. Having said that, I cannot tell you the guilt I feel at having placed you in this onerous position. I wouldn't have wished it on my worst enemy.

'Once Uncle Caputo learns what has happened he will lose no time in tracking you down. Whatever happens we must find Caterina first. At least we know what we are looking for. There can't be many girls in convent school uniform loose in Paris. It can only be a matter of time.'

'Aah!' It was Monsieur Pamplemousse's turn to drain his glass. 'We may have a problem there, *Monsieur*. It depends what she is wearing. It could be either one of two extremes.'

He picked up the envelope the receptionist had given him and carefully unwound the string fastening the flap. Trigaux had certainly excelled himself. It was packed with glossy 20 cm × 25 cm prints. He must have dropped everything. Perhaps the subject matter had appealed to him.

'These are some photographs I took on the journey.'

Removing them, he flipped through the pile. Most of the earlier ones were of Pommes Frites: Pommes Frites gazing out of the hotel window; Pommes Frites chasing a Roman pigeon; Pommes Frites waiting patiently outside the Vatican, looking as though he might be hoping for an audience with the Pope.

The photographs he was searching for were at the end of the pile. Apart from the colour prints of those taken inside the Termini at Rome, where he could have done with a faster film, they looked sharp enough. The ones taken on the train were on black and white stock and bore all the hallmarks of a flash photograph; hard shadows, lack of facial tones, but they were pleasing nevertheless. Although he said it himself, they wouldn't have disgraced the pages of many a fashion magazine.

'These are the snaps I was looking for, *Monsieur*. As you will see, they show two different sides of your niece – before and after as it were.'

The Director sat bolt upright in his chair. 'Before and after what, Pamplemousse?' he exclaimed. 'What are you trying to tell me?'

It was Monsieur Pamplemousse's turn to ignore the interruption. 'The first two were taken when your *petite cousine* arrived at *la gare*, *Monsieur*. The rest were taken on the Palatino after she had changed for *dîner*.'

As he glanced at the photographs, the remaining colour drained from the Director's face.

'This is terrible, Pamplemousse. Much worse than I believed possible. I would hardly call them *snaps*.'

'They were intended as a surprise, *Monsieur*.'

'They are more than that, Pamplemousse. They are a severe shock. I can hardly believe my eyes.'

'I have to admit I was somewhat taken aback myself, *Monsieur*. It was a total transformation.'

'Where were the later pictures taken, Pamplemousse?'

'She was sitting on the bed in my compartment.'

The Director clutched the side of his chair. 'I feared as much.'

'There is no cause for alarm, *Monsieur*. I can assure you it is not how it looks. The door was open at all times. The compartments are very small and I had to stand in the corridor in order to achieve a pleasing composition. There was an American couple in the one next to mine. I remember the first flash made them jump. There is also the conductor. He made up a bed for Pommes Frites and received a handsome *pourboire* for his trouble . . .'

Monsieur Pamplemousse's voice trailed away. The conductor was one witness he would never be able to call on. He wondered if he should tell the Director what had happened to the man, then thought better of it.

'Pamplemousse, this story must never, ever reach the ears of others.'

'Least of all the Mother Superior?' hazarded Monsieur Pamplemousse.

'It is not the Mother Superior I am worried about,' said the Director. 'It is Uncle Rocco.'

'There is no earthly reason why he should ever know, *Monsieur*.'

'What if the person operating the processing machine took a fancy to the pictures and had copies made?'

'I hardly think that is likely, *Monsieur*.' Trigaux's last words to him had been 'Don't tell the chief – he's having a purge on home processing. Madame Grante's been getting at him.' He couldn't let him down.

'You do not know, Pamplemousse. You do not know. It is not beyond the bounds of possibility that the conces sionaires are already paying some form of protection money – "insurance" against unforeseen dilution of their chemicals en route from the factory. Not necessarily to Uncle Caputo – it is not his territory – but to the member of another family.'

'This is France, *Monsieur*, not Sicily.'

The Director looked less than convinced. 'I trust these are the only pictures you took? You are not hiding anything?'

'What are you suggesting, *Monsieur*? You surely don't think ... Caterina is young enough to be my daughter – my granddaughter even. What I have told you is the simple truth.'

'The truth is seldom simple, Aristide, and it often has as many faces as there are those involved. I do not doubt your version of the affair, or that your intentions were entirely honourable. Doubtless, if you asked Caterina for her opinion, she would see it in an entirely different light.

'However, what you or I think is immaterial. It is what Uncle Rocco thinks that matters. I am simply placing myself in his shoes. Shoes, Pamplemousse, purchased from Salvatore Ferragamo in Florence and polished with the blood of those who have offended him along the way; burnished until they could have seen their own faces in them had they still been alive to do so, and always assuming they would have wished to see their faces after he had finished with them.

'I know the way his mind works. There you are in Rome, meeting his only beloved daughter – a girl still at convent school. Within an hour you have persuaded her to dress in a manner which would not have passed unnoticed on the stage of the *Folies Bergère*. You then take her to the buffet car and ply her with drink.'

'It would have seemed churlish not to have offered her any liquid refreshment, *Monsieur*. I felt sure you would wish me to.'

'There are other beverages, Pamplemousse. Some form of Cola might have been preferable in the circumstances.'

Monsieur Pamplemousse felt for his notebook. 'I kept a strict record, *Monsieur* . . .'

The Director raised his hand. 'Wait, I have not yet finished. I am merely seeing things through Uncle Rocco's eyes. Having plied his only daughter with drink, you take her back to your compartment and there you persuade her to pose in a most provocative manner. Shortly afterwards you ask the attendant to make up another bed, offering the lame excuse that it is for your dog. On your own admission you offered the man a sum of money, presumably to make sure his lips were sealed. Doubtless the same couple who were startled by your flash witnessed you doing that too.

'Try convincing Uncle Rocco it was all done in pure innocence. You will soon see why he deserves the nickname "Caputo".'

'It shows a great lack of faith in his daughter, *Monsieur*.'

'It shows a great lack of faith in human nature, Pamplemousse, but where he comes from faith in human nature lies thinly on the ground, usually surmounted by a cross to show where it died. Uncle Rocco's reasoning would be that it is not simply a case of Caterina exchanging her dark blue bloomers with double gussets for frilly garments of a more provocative kind. If you think what that prospect does to others, think what it must also do to the wearer. A wearer, moreover, who is doubtless still suffering from having once already reached out to pluck the forbidden fruit, only to feel it literally slip from her grasp. Whatever the outcome of this sad affair, the fact remains that in his eyes you have condemned her to eternal damnation and there is no going back.

'Now, to cap everything, you have lost her and she is all alone in a strange city. The heady rush of Parisian air in her nostrils may well have brought on an attack of amnesia, leaving her unable to make up her mind which way to turn. I need hardly remind you, Pamplemousse, that the streets of Paris are filled with those who will be only too willing to guide her.'

Gloom settled over the Director again. 'You know what this means, of course?'

Monsieur Pamplemousse shook his head.

'You must go to ground, Pamplemousse, possibly never to emerge.'

'But why me, *Monsieur*?'

'Because, Pamplemousse, as soon as Uncle Rocco hears the news you will be seen as the prime suspect and he will go for the jugular.'

'But, *Monsieur*, I have already said I can explain everything...'

'Explanations,' said the Director heavily, 'do not come easy when you are standing at the bottom of the Seine wearing nothing but a pair of concrete boots. "Thinks balloons" will emerge as bubbles. You see now why I said we cannot possibly go to the police. No-one must know what has happened. I will stay here and man the fort, staving off all questions to the best of my ability.

'Your only hope – your only salvation – lies in finding Caterina with all possible speed. In the meantime you must make yourself as scarce as possible.'

It didn't escape Monsieur Pamplemousse's notice that the two tasks were not exactly compatible, nor did he fail to observe that the Director was already distancing himself from the affair. The word 'you' was starting to appear with alarming regularity.

'I will instruct Véronique to light a candle for you in the church of St Pierre du Gros Caillou.' As the Director picked up the phone, he felt in his pocket, then he appeared to change his mind. 'I shall also warn Chantal not to return to Paris until I give her the all-clear. I suggest you make similar arrangements with your own wife.'

While he was talking, the Director turned and crossed once again to his French windows, there to gaze silently at the lowering sky. It was a clear signal, if one were needed, that conversation was at an end.

Imbued with a sense of impending doom, Monsieur Pamplemousse made his way slowly out of the room, closely followed by Pommes Frites, his tail hanging at a suitably recumbent angle.

Véronique was already taking the Director's call. '*Oui, Monsieur*, I will make sure it is carried out straight away.

67

Oui, Monsieur, I will arrange for a candle to be lit. The ten-franc size? *Oui*, I will take it out of petty cash.'

As Monsieur Pamplemousse passed her desk she placed her other hand over the mouthpiece of the receiver. She looked in a state of shock.

'*Monsieur* . . . I had no idea . . .'

'It happens . . .' Monsieur Pamplemousse didn't know what to say.

Véronique looked as though she would either burst into tears at any moment or start organising a collection on his behalf. Either way it was no time to linger.

As he left the building Monsieur Pamplemousse paused, unsure for the moment which way to go; whether to take his car or walk for a while. Suddenly feeling very alone, he looked round to make sure Pommes Frites was still with him. He also couldn't help but wonder how long a ten-franc candle normally lasted. A day? Two days? Knowing the ways of the Vatican, probably a lot less. To the best of his knowledge the church of St Pierre du Gros Caillou was used by Ukrainians, but at least it was fairly near the office.

It didn't add to his peace of mind that on the way out he had called in at the Operations room: that sacred part of the building where, day and night, uniformed girls armed with long poles kept constant vigil on the whereabouts of all the Inspectors, manoeuvring their personal figurines around a table-top map of France with croupier-like efficiency as they up-dated their every movement.

His own figurine had already been relegated to a parking bay near the back; somewhere on the outskirts of Lille.

4

THE SEARCH BEGINS

A feeling of *déjà vu* came over Monsieur Pamplemousse as he arrived back at his apartment. The telephone was ringing again. This time he decided to ignore it. If it was the Director with more prophecies of doom he didn't wish to know. If it was anyone else they could wait. First things first. Number one priority was a stiff drink. Brillat-Savarin had never spoken a truer word when he said that man is the only creature who drinks when he is not thirsty.

He poured himself a large cognac. After the earlier Roullet it tasted like firewater. *Très Rare Hors d'Age* was not what it was all about. When all this was over – *if* it was ever over – he would remind the Director that a bottle of his favourite cognac wouldn't look out of place in the drinks cabinet *chez* Pamplemousse. In the circumstances it was the least Monsieur Leclercq could do.

After a moment or two Monsieur Pamplemousse reached for the telephone and dialled a Melun number. He drew the short straw. Doucette's sister answered.

'Agathe. How are you?' He immediately regretted asking. Agathe was the kind of person whose health one didn't enquire after. It was her favourite subject. Visits to the doctor were seldom undertaken without her taking along a wall chart showing all the organs of the female body – in full colour.

Cupping the receiver under his left ear, Monsieur Pamplemousse reached for the envelope he had brought back from the office and emptied the contents on to the table. Spreading the photographs out across its surface, he began sorting through them, putting the earlier ones – mostly of Pommes Frites – to one side in order to concentrate his attention on the last reel. He had said it before and he would say it again – Trigaux had done a good job. It was easy to see why. The Director's *petite cousine* must have made a pleasant change from endless shots showing the outside of hotels.

There was no doubt Caterina was beautiful. She had a haunting quality. She would go places, of that he was sure. There was a determined look in her eyes. But wasn't there something else as well? Another, deeper layer. A vulnerability perhaps, or an innocence? Perhaps in the end she was a flawed beauty? It was hard to say which element lay just beneath the surface and which was on top. The various sides of her character seemed inextricably mixed up; each one trying to fight its way out. But wasn't that the case with most teenagers?

And had there not been, in that brief moment when she had suddenly and unexpectedly kissed him in the train, an exchange of something else again? It had nothing to do with giving or taking, or of expecting anything in return. It had simply been a brief and uncomplicated moment of truth; the sharing of a secret, as with a brother and sister. Or perhaps more appositely in this case, between father and daughter. A bond had been forged, like the wiping of a pin-prick of blood on to the paper image of a saint in a Mafia initiation ceremony, and he knew that whatever happened, if Caterina were in trouble he would go to her aid without question.

'*Chérie.*' Monsieur Pamplemousse suddenly realised Doucette was talking to him. It was a good thing videophones were still a thing of the future. 'Have you been trying to get me? A moment ago . . . ?

'*Non*? I simply wondered, that is all. The phone was ringing when I came in . . .

'*Non.* I have been at the office. Pommes Frites and I had a good *déjeuner.* Too much . . . I am afraid we went to sleep afterwards. I would have telephoned before, but something urgent has cropped up at work. It always happens near publication time.'

Monsieur Pamplemousse hesitated, wondering how best to frame what he wanted to say. In the event the problem was solved without his having to say a word. Doucette was the one who sounded worried; more on his behalf than her own.

'*Couscous*, of course I do not mind if you stay the night. Stay for as long as you wish. I shall be busy for the rest of the week . . .'

He hoped he hadn't sounded too relieved, too anxious to fall in with her plans. Doucette had a keen ear for undue emphasis; the unnecessary underlining of words in what was intended to be taken merely as a casual remark. Out of context, such utterances didn't always stand up to close analysis. Her next question realised his worst fears.

'*Monsieur le Directeur's petite cousine?* Poof! She is but a child.'

Monsieur Pamplemousse cast his eyes around the room and settled on a photograph of his sister-in-law. 'I fear nature has not been kind to her, *Couscous*. She is grossly overweight and much given to complaining.'

'Oh dear, Aristide, did you have a very tedious time?' Doucette sounded contrite. He must have struck a sympathetic chord. No doubt she was suffering too.

'I would rather not talk about it, *chérie* . . .

'*Oui.* I will telephone in the morning. I may know more of what is happening then. *Monsieur le Directeur* is up to his eyes at present.

'You, too. Sleep well!'

Monsieur Pamplemousse replaced the receiver rather quicker than he had intended. He hoped it hadn't sounded too abrupt. He sat for a moment or two lost in thought. It was good that Doucette had opted to stay with her sister. It was one less thing to worry about. Judging from the tone of the conversation, if Agathe had any say in the matter – which she undoubtedly would – he might be on his own for several days.

His mind returned to the events at the Gare de Lyon. How was it that the man on the Palatino had been there too? Had he also been looking for Caterina? Even more to the point – had he been responsible for the death of the conductor? The more he turned the matter over in his mind, the more certain Monsieur Pamplemousse felt it was a self-answering question. The evidence was purely circumstantial, of course – it wouldn't stand up for a second in a court of law. But it was too much of a coincidence for there to be any other explanation.

But why? What possible reason could there have been for murder? It couldn't have been a premeditated act.

He rose to his feet and crossed to the French windows. Opening them, he went out on to the small balcony which ran the length of the building. Ciné 13 on the corner of rue Junot must be holding a private screening, for there were people in evening dress gathered outside. He could hear their chatter and the occasional shrill laugh. A pair of lovers stopped to watch, probably hoping to catch a glimpse of someone famous.

Across to its left, beyond the old Moulin de la Galette and further down the hill, he could see the large shape of the Cimetière de Montmartre, where he and Pommes Frites had walked earlier in the day; an island of darkness now, submerged in a sea of twinkling lights. The resident population of cats would be on the prowl by now, safe from the likes of Pommes Frites.

To its left, the sky was illuminated by the glow from the Place de Clichy; an amalgam of multi-coloured neon signs and light from restaurants and cinemas, criss-crossed by headlights from a never-ending stream of traffic flowing in all directions. The view across the rooftops was one of his favourites – at any time of the day or night. But night-time brought its own magic, glossing over some of the less salubrious aspects of the area.

On the lower slopes of Montmartre – the one-time hill of windmills – the hookers would be out in force, watched over by their pimps. *Racoleurs* would be trying to entice likely-looking candidates into the strip joints in order to make their percentage on the grossly overpriced drinks. Concierges in the rue de Douai would be handing out 'short-time keys' on a strictly cash in advance basis.

In the far distance, beyond Place de Clichy, he could make out the Eiffel Tower, and to its right the Arc de Triomphe. Beyond that lay the whole of western France, and then the Mediterranean. And beyond that again, lay Sicily with its strange medieval, closed-in society from which there was no escape, and its family feuds which bubbled away over the centuries, occasionally erupting like a volcano into unbelievably savage and bloody acts of revenge. Sicily, with its code of *omertà* – its conspiracy of silence – a code enforced in the old days by sawn-off shotguns, and nowadays by the short-barrelled .38 or Magnum .357 armed with exploding bullets.

Sicily and Uncle Caputo. The name, in the circumstances, sounded more fitting than Rocco.

And now, somewhere in amongst the teeming mass of humanity that went to make up Paris, was Uncle Caputo's daughter, alone and unprotected. The Director was right. If anything happened to Caterina he, Aristide Pamplemousse, would be held responsible.

Retribution would be a foregone conclusion; swift in its execution – terrible in its method. Monsieur Pamplemousse had no wish to end his days trussed-up like a goat in the boot of a car, legs doubled back behind him, feet lashed together with the other end of the rope tied round his neck. If he didn't die by self-strangulation, he would be shot in the back of the head prior to being fed to the pigs, or liquefied in a barrel of acid which would later be poured down a drain. When the Mafia used the words like 'erase' or 'remove' they weren't joking. They called it the 'white death'.

He might, of course, be left to simmer for a while. Since

it was a question of someone else's territory, a contract would have to be negotiated, and that in turn would be followed by weeks of never leaving the apartment without wondering whether it was for the last time. Until the day came when he got careless...

A flash of unseasonable lightning lit up the sky towards the eastern outskirts of Paris, momentarily silhouetting the massive skyscrapers of La Défence.

Monsieur Pamplemousse shivered as he turned to go back inside. Finding Caterina had to be number one priority and time was not on his side. As he closed the French windows he heard the sound of thunder rolling away in the distance.

Crossing to the hi-fi he slipped a tape into the cassette player: *Ellington and Friends*. The soothing strains of Mood Indigo filled the room. He poured himself another cognac. It was a time for firewater; a time for action.

Pull yourself together, Pamplemousse. Facts. You are not entirely without facts. You must marshal them. Put them into some kind of order. Seating himself at the table once again, he reached for his pen and began writing on the back of Trigaux's envelope – making out a list, as he so often did at such times, of the pros and cons. It helped concentrate his thoughts.

You have acquired a little knowledge of the girl. You spent one entire meal with her and you have been privileged to talk with her in a way that perhaps few others have, and to learn something about her.

You know she has ambitions to be a model. Presumably that is the real reason why she wished to come to Paris. But why Paris? Why not Rome? Rome would be too close to home. From all she had said, *papà* would certainly not approve. And now that he knew *papà's* identity he could well understand her fears.

Assuming for the moment that she had set off of her own accord, where would she head for? Where would she start? One of the big model agencies? One of the well-known fashion photographers? Perhaps, like the girl she had mentioned – Naomi something – Campbell? – at the door of some glossy magazine.

Hoping for inspiration, Monsieur Pamplemousse picked up the telephone directory and began flipping through the pages. He quickly abandoned the idea. There were model agencies galore. Photographers occupied several pages. He looked up *journaux*. There were so many he didn't know where to begin. He would need help to go through them all. If he followed that line of thought he would have to go knocking on a great many doors.

But then so would Caterina. Almost certainly she would start at the top. In that respect at least she would have a head start. Clearly she knew exactly what was what in matters of fashion. His own knowledge – at least as far as women's wear was concerned – could have been written on the back of a postage stamp. It was another world.

On the other hand, he did have her likeness. Not an end of term school photograph – although in a sense he had that too – but one which showed a totally different side to her. One which any agency or dress designer would recognise immediately if she had paid them a call.

Working his way back through the pile in chronological order he reached the ones taken in the Stazione Termini in Rome. Suddenly he paused.

Opening up his issue case from *Le Guide*, he took out a

magnifying glass and focused on a picture showing a general view of the main concourse. Luckily it was one he had taken before boarding the train – almost the last of a reel of colour film. After that he had changed to black and white and it might have escaped his attention.

Immediately in front of the departure board there was a small, red triangular telephone booth – one of a number dotted about the area. As with Caterina's hat, it stood out amongst the surrounding tones of black and grey like a sore thumb. Occupying a booth nearest to the lens was the ubiquitous Il Blobbo. He had a receiver to his ear, but clearly he was more interested in watching the passing crowd than in whoever it was he was talking to; if, indeed, he was carrying on a conversation at all. The thin-rimmed dark glasses were what gave him away. The same dark glasses he had last seen lying on the track alongside the conductor in *quai* 'J' at the Gare de Lyon.

It confirmed his worst fears.

What was it the Director had said? 'I need hardly remind you, Pamplemousse, that the streets of Paris are filled with those who will be only too willing to guide her . . .'

Supposing it hadn't started in the streets of Paris. Supposing it had begun much earlier. On the night train from Rome, *par exemple*?

The more he thought about it, the more convinced Monsieur Pamplemousse became that he was right. It would also account for Caterina's reserve on the subject when she had been talking to him. Women – girls – tough though they could be in many respects, could also be surprisingly naïve at times. Perhaps 'trusting' was a better word. You only had to read the *journaux*. Perhaps it had to do with wish-fulfilment. Caterina's desire to become a model might well have outweighed her common sense.

One thing was certain. If it was the man on the Palatino there was no knowing where she might end up. It certainly wouldn't be on the catwalk at a fashion show. He wouldn't have trusted the man any further than he could have thrown him, and subsequent events seemed to bear that out.

Crossing to the cassette player, Monsieur Pamplemousse stopped the tape and slipped it back into its case. 'Sophisticated Lady' was hardly a suitable refrain in the circumstances.

He picked up the telephone.

Despite his promise to the Director, there were times when you needed the help of the professionals, and this was one of them. Without giving away his true reason for asking, there would be no harm in putting out a few feelers.

He dialled the number of the *Sûreté* and asked to be put through to his old department.

Luck was with him. Ex-colleague and friend, Jacques, was working late.

'Aristide! *Comment ça va?*'

'*Bien, merci. Et vous?*'

Jacques sounded pleased to be interrupted. He regaled Monsieur Pamplemousse with a list of reasons before getting down to routine inquiries.

'Doucette?' Monsieur Pamplemousse hesitated. 'She is well. She is staying with her sister in Melun for a few days.' Now that he had the floor, so to speak, he looked for a way to justify his reason for calling.

'I was wondering if you can help me. I am doing an article on prostitution for the Staff magazine . . .

'*Oui*, I know *Le Guide* is to do with food, but there are other appetites which often go hand in hand . . .

'*Non*, I would rather not talk to anyone in the vice squad for the moment.

'*Non*, nor anyone in the Brigade for the Repression of Pimping. In my day they did not have such a body.' Having lit the fuse, he paused for Jacques to begin. He hadn't long to wait. Clearly it was a subject close to his heart.

'The vice squad is run by a woman these days. Mme Martine Monteuil: ex-drug squad with the smashing of a Chinese heroin racket to her credit before she became Paris's only female police *commissaire*. I wouldn't like to get on the wrong side of her.'

Monsieur Pamplemousse could almost sense Jacques looking apprehensively over his shoulder. He had read about Mme Monteuil. Elegance personified. The Hermès scarf; the fashionably short skirt; the classic quilted Chanel shoulder-bag housing not a powder compact, but a .357 Magnum. By all accounts she was ready to use it, too.

'Mind you,' said Jacques, 'if you want my opinion, at the end of the day she's on to a losing battle. You don't always have the sympathy of the hierarchy behind you, let alone the public. The rue St Denis without its women would be like cheese without wine, and most of them are a mine of information. Remember the last big raid there?'

Monsieur Pamplemousse did. In addition to a varied selection of pimps, prostitutes and clients, the police had netted three of their own senior officers, all of whom had

claimed they were involved in secret undercover operations. Under the bedcover operations more like it.

'You're right in your equation,' said Jacques. 'There
are two things that are always going to be in demand –
food and sex. And when you really get down to it people
can go without food for a long time. Prostitution is the
only business in France that doesn't shut down for
August. Close down one area in Paris and it soon opens
up again in another.'

'So what's new?' asked Monsieur Pamplemousse.

Jacques considered the question for all of three
seconds. 'Not much has really changed since your time.
Shifting Les Halles out to Rungis caused a big upheaval,
as you can imagine. Taxis are out – the girls have taken to
waiting at the exits to the *Périphérique* with their
caravanettes. Most of the old *hôtels de passe* have been
shut down, and there's even a trade union now: the
Association d'Action et de Défense des Prostitutées they
call it.'

'How about brothels?'

'Well, as you know, prostitution is still legal – provided
you aren't caught moving while you tout for custom.
Brothels aren't, so those who run them go to great lengths
to trade under another name – they're much more
discreet these days. They're called *clandés* and most of
them have a little plaque by the door saying "Villa –" or
"*Résidence* whatever". There was a case in the 15th not
long ago. A certain Mme Zabbel set up a charity for what
she called the "Association for Happy Animals". Her first
big mistake was putting a brass plate up outside her house
announcing the fact. All the kids and old ladies in the
neighbourhood turned up with stray pets they'd come

across. Her second mistake was going on television – one of the vice squad recognised her as someone he'd arrested years before for the same thing . . .'

'Any other areas I need to know about?'

'Minitels are the "in" thing nowadays. There's no need to go out any more – you just tap out the options on a screen. The PTT are making a fortune, but nobody gets them for living off immoral earnings. There was even a case of a call-girl operation being run on a church computer under the guise of a share-dealing service . . .

'Of course, if you're doing an article on vice you can't leave out the gay bars and clubs – the rue Sainte-Anne is lined with them. Or there are the *boîtes à partouze* – the clubs for mass sex – there's one on the rue de Chazelle. Massage parlours, escort services – you name it.

'Then there's the Bois de Boulogne, but that's been cleaned up ever since the boys from the Salubrité du Bois de Boulogne moved in. At one time you could hardly move at night for all the *travelos* – transvestites, trans-sexuals out walking their dogs hoping to rake in enough dough to pay for a sex change operation in Morocco – not to mention the ones who'd turned up to watch.'

Monsieur Pamplemousse suppressed a smile. That was one area he wouldn't have to bother with. He felt sure Caterina would be perfectly happy to stay the way nature had intended her to be, thank you very much.

'How about the pimps themselves?' He broke in while he had the chance. Jacques sounded as though he had settled down for the rest of the evening.

'They're having a harder time. The Eric Botey's of this world – remember him? He used to run that chain of hotels in Pigalle – they've mostly gone. The ones that are left go in for real estate – renting "studios" they call it, at prices only someone on the game could afford. On top of that they use hot-dog salesmen with their street barrows to keep an eye on the comings and goings – just so they don't lose out on their percentage. They don't miss a trick – if you'll pardon the pun.'

'Where would the youngest and newest girls be found?'

Monsieur Pamplemousse thought he detected a slight hesitation at the other end. 'Luxury or cheap? *Comme ci – comme ça*. Avenue Foch or rue de la Goutte-d'Or? It depends on what you want. There are always new ones arriving. Look round any main-line station.'

'How about the trains themselves?' Monsieur Pamplemousse broke in again.

'I haven't come across it, but it wouldn't surprise me. Since I did an attachment to the vice squad nothing surprises me. It might be a good way of picking out likely candidates without running the risk of being jumped on.'

'The sort of girl I am looking for,' said Monsieur Pamplemousse, 'would be young, still at school – a Catholic girls' school – she would have blue eyes, dark hair . . .'

'*Oh, là, là!*' A whistle assailed his left ear. 'She could name her own price. If you go up the social ladder a rung or two then things work in a different way. At the top there are always people willing and able to pay for the best. It depends on what your tastes are.'

'I am not asking how much,' said Monsieur Pamplemousse. 'I am simply asking where?'

'Money no object, eh? Things must be good in the restaurant business. Is it the seven-year itch?'

'Hardly. I have been married twenty-eight years.'

'The very worst. That's the four-times factor. You must have got it badly.'

'Now look here . . .'

'How long did you say Doucette's away for? I must say you don't waste any time.'

Monsieur Pamplemousse took a deep breath while he counted up to ten. Talk about giving a dog a bad name. Any moment now he would be reminded of the affair at the *Folies* – the scandal that had forced his early retirement. No doubt the number of girls credited with being involved had risen with the years.

'If you want my advice, old man, you'll stick at home with a good book. It's much safer these days.'

Sensing that Jacques was about to terminate the conversation, Monsieur Pamplemousse tried another tack.

'Before you go,' he said, 'there was a murder at the Gare de Lyon earlier this evening . . . I think I may be able to help.'

'We already have a description of the man we want,' said Jacques. 'Middle-aged. Height around 170, maybe 175 centimetres. Weight around 100 kilogrammes. Small moustache. Fresh complexion. Wearing an overcoat and a brown hat – or it may have been black.'

'Or green?' suggested Monsieur Pamplemousse. 'Or red?'

'I know, I know,' said Jacques. 'But he had a large dog with him. That may help. They're making up an identikit picture of the man right now. I'm waiting for it to be sent up.'

'And the dog?' asked Monsieur Pamplemousse drily. 'Are they doing one of him too?'

'The consensus of opinion is that it was a Great Dane.'

'The real culprit,' said Monsieur Pamplemousse, 'was totally unlike the person you describe. I can provide you with a photograph, if you like – in colour.'

It did the trick. Jacques was suddenly all ears.

'You were there?'

'As it happens . . . by sheer coincidence . . .

'*Oui*. I will be at the Quai des Orfèvres as soon as possible.'

Monsieur Pamplemousse had hardly replaced the receiver when the phone rang again. This time he answered it.

'*Allo. Allo. Qui est là?*' There was a moment's silence. In the background he could hear the sound of traffic and an engine revving, as though the driver was anxious to be on his way. Then, whoever was making the call hung up.

Monsieur Pamplemousse sat staring at the instrument for a moment or two, wondering if his caller would try again. Then he got up and wandered round the apartment, automatically straightening a picture here, aligning a row of books along the edge of a shelf there, thumbing through some old *journaux*.

Pommes Frites followed him with his eyes. He knew the signs of old. His master had a problem and there wouldn't be much rest until he had solved it. He wondered what it was this time.

Having turned out the light, Monsieur Pamplemousse opened the French windows again and went outside on to the balcony. Pommes Frites padded silently after him and peered through the grille of the iron balustrade. Suddenly he stiffened and a low growl issued from the depths of his stomach.

Monsieur Pamplemousse registered the fact. It was a note of warning; a signal that something was bothering him. He followed the direction of Pommes Frites' gaze along the street, but there was nothing to be seen. Rue Girardon was unusually empty, perhaps because of the passing storm. A car swept past and turned into rue Junot. The cobblestones glistened in the headlamps and there was a hiss from the tyres. It must have been raining hard while he had been inside.

Another flash of lightning lit up the street, and he saw a man approaching alongside the gardens opposite. He was wearing a dark overcoat and he was breathing heavily as though he had just completed the long climb up the steps from rue Caulaincourt. The thunder was nearer this time: almost overhead. As the sound died away the man stopped beneath a lamp and glanced up – either at the sky or at the apartment block – it was hard to say which.

Monsieur Pamplemousse stepped back into the shadows to await developments. Was he letting his imagination run away with him, or was it not the third time that day he had seen the man? And had the last occasion not been at the Gare de Lyon, moments after the Palatino had left for Rome?

Clearly, from the way he was reacting, Pommes Frites thought so too, and he was rarely wrong about such matters.

And if that were the case . . . If that were the case it meant the man hadn't been at the *gare* by accident. The possibility that someone might be tailing him hadn't crossed Monsieur Pamplemousse's mind at the time – either in the taxi to the office or on the journey home. Nor had it when he responded to the Director's call. His mind had been so busy with other things, he had paid little or no attention to the traffic behind.

There was another possibility, of course. He had given Caterina a card with his home address. Could she have passed it on – either voluntarily or for some other more sinister reason?

Putting a finger to his mouth for Pommes Frites' benefit, Monsieur Pamplemousse retreated slowly into the living-room and once he was inside, drew the curtains on all the windows. Only after he had made absolutely certain there were no cracks where the folds met did he turn on the light.

Then he rang the Quai des Orfèvres and asked for Jacques.

'On second thoughts, would it be possible for you to come here?

'You know what it's like in Montmartre at night. You take your car out and you lose your parking space until early next morning.'

It was a truthful statement of fact. If he omitted to say that he had an arrangement with the owners of the block next door which gave him off-street parking facilities, that was simply because it was something he wished to keep to himself for the time being.

Jacques sounded pleased to have an excuse to get out of the office for a while. He bucked up even more when asked if he felt hungry.

'I was about to go to the canteen!'

Making his way into the kitchen, Monsieur Pamplemousse opened the refrigerator door. The food Doucette had left was sitting in its polythene wrapping. So was the small package of truffles he'd brought back from Italy.

Allowing for clearing up his desk and issuing orders for a car, it would be at least twenty minutes before Jacques reached him. Fresh truffles were best eaten as soon as possible. It would be a shame if he allowed them to spoil.

Twenty minutes later Monsieur Pamplemousse tested the potatoes with a sharp-pointed knife. It slid in easily. Draining the water into the sink, he replaced the saucepan on the hob for a second or two to dry out the remains of the liquid before turning off the gas. Then he dropped several small knobs of butter on to the potatoes and as they started to melt, added a little milk, followed by a sprinkling of black pepper and some grated nutmeg. He began mashing the contents of the saucepan with a fork; gently, for he wanted to preserve a slight coarseness rather than end up with *pommes purée*. He was in the middle of the operation when he heard the sound of an approaching siren coming up rue Junot from the direction of Clichy.

Emptying the mixture on to a board, he picked up a palette knife and quickly moulded the potato into four generous-sized portions. Removing the truffles from the glass of cognac where they had been resting, he reached for a *mandoline* and began slicing them thinly and cleanly until they covered the top of all four cakes. The smell which rose as the heat from the potatoes permeated the truffles was earthy and good; like no other smell in the world.

He was only just in time. As he reached for the pepper pot again the buzzer on the entry-phone sounded and there was a crackle followed by a metallic voice over the intercom. Putting the plates under a gentle grill to keep warm, Monsieur Pamplemousse acknowledged the call, pressed the lock release button for the downstairs door and poured two glasses of wine from an opened bottle of Guigal '78 Côte Rotie 'Brune et Blonde'. It was the last but one in a case he'd bought *en primeur* when it became available – one of Bernard's bargain offers. Fortunately for his colleagues Bernard had never entirely severed his earlier connections with the wine trade. Long may it remain that way!

The sound of the lift coming to a halt in the corridor outside the apartment and then footsteps, followed by the strident noise of the door buzzer, sent Pommes Frites hurrying to the entrance hall. He stood waiting expectantly, his body taut and ready for action.

Following on behind, Monsieur Pamplemousse placed his hand on the door knob and was about to slip the catch when some sixth sense, honed razor sharp through years in the force, caused him to pause. He flashed a brief signal with his eyes to Pommes Frites. It was received and understood in a flash.

'*Attaquez! Attaquez!*'

Shouting out the words, Monsieur Pamplemousse flung open the door and flattened himself against the wall as some 50 kilos of unstoppable muscle, bone and flesh shot past him into the hall. There followed a brief, but satisfactory crash, and then silence.

5

CATCH 22

'*Merde!* What was all that about?' Jacques looked aggrieved, as well he might. Having had what felt like a lump of living, breathing concrete suddenly land on his chest when he least expected it was no laughing matter. It was a case of Greek meeting Greek, for Jacques was no lightweight. Pommes Frites was looking distinctly sorry for himself too.

Monsieur Pamplemousse tried to pass it off. 'It doesn't do to take chances these days. You said so yourself.'

'That was different.' Jacques glanced around for somewhere to hang his hat. As he did so he spotted a clothes' brush.

Keeping a respectful distance from Pommes Frites, who was clearly only waiting for an opportunity to lick him better, he followed Monsieur Pamplemousse into the living room, tidying himself up as he went.

'It's not like you to be jumpy. Does everyone get the same treatment?'

'Come, I will show you why.' Monsieur Pamplemousse

went through the routine of turning out the lights and drawing the curtains back. He opened the French windows and led the way out on to the balcony. Anxious to make amends, Pommes Frites pushed his way to the front and peered down at the street. His tail dropped several degrees as it registered disappointment.

Monsieur Pamplemousse looked first towards the far corner of the tiny square Marcel Aymé. It was the obvious place to stand if anyone wanted to keep an eye on the comings and goings of the apartment block, for it was possible to see along both sides, but there was no one around. The crowd outside the cinema had long since dispersed.

The other streets in the surrounding area looked unusually deserted for a Friday night; he drew a blank in all directions. The storm must have driven everyone away. The only sign of anything untoward was a white car parked facing the wrong way on the other side of the road. Even without the blue light attached to the roof it wouldn't have been hard to guess who it belonged to.

'Well? I hope you didn't make me come all the way across Paris simply to admire the view?' Jacques sounded as though insult had been added to injury.

'I think perhaps it was a mistake to use the siren.'

Jacques shrugged. 'They always do in *Miami Vice*. Besides, you made it sound urgent.'

'They do lots of strange things in *Miami Vice*,' said Monsieur Pamplemousse gruffly. All the same, he took the point. It was catching. No-one in the force went anywhere these days without a siren. In his time it had been a case of 'softly, softly, catchee monkey'.

Ushering Jacques back into the apartment, he drew the

curtains and felt for the light switch. He wasn't an illusionist; staring into the night wouldn't make anyone appear if they weren't there to begin with – or were making sure they were nowhere to be seen. All the same, it was disappointing.

'Pour yourself some wine.' Monsieur Pamplemousse motioned Jacques to take a seat at the table while he hurried out into the kitchen.

'Don't tell me . . .' The smell as he opened the warming compartment of the oven must have penetrated into the other room, for he heard the other's voice.

'Diamonds of the kitchen!' Jacques eyed the plates as Monsieur Pamplemousse returned. 'I can't remember when I last had any. Certainly not so as you can't see what's underneath.'

'It is the only way,' said Monsieur Pamplemousse simply. 'Let us not waste time. They've been kept hanging about too long already.'

'Whose fault is that?' Jacques smacked his lips. 'There's nothing like a good peasant dish to round off the day. When I was a boy we had them every Sunday. Truffle omelette before the main course. In those days it was easier to find the truffles than the eggs. Now look at the price.'

'F3,800 francs a kilo in Fauchon,' said Monsieur Pamplemousse.

'Everything's F3,800 francs a kilo in Fauchon.' Jacques raised his glass and gave an appreciative sniff.

'How the poor do live!'

The truffles were still beautifully fresh and crunchy; the Côte Rotie a perfect match. In its own way, it was equally earthy; powerful as the Rhône valley itself, with a fruity, fig-like flavour, combined with a wonderfully dry finish.

For a moment or two they ate and drank in silence. It would have been sacrilege to do anything else.

'So, what can you tell me about the stiff at the Gare de Lyon?' Jacques wiped his plate clean as a whistle, glanced hopefully towards the kitchen, then helped himself to some more wine.

Monsieur Pamplemousse pushed the photograph he had taken of the main concourse at the Stazione Termini across the table.

'That's your man. I would stake my life on it.' He indicated the telephone kiosk with his forefinger. 'The one with the dark glasses.'

Jacques stared at it dubiously. 'You're sure it's not a fly?'

Monsieur Pamplemousse rose from the table and returned a moment later with the magnifying glass. 'Try that.'

Pushing aside his wine glass with a certain amount of reluctance, Jacques picked up the photograph and held it to the light. Then he felt inside his jacket and withdrew a folded sheet of A4 paper and made a show of comparing the two.

Glancing over the other's shoulder, Monsieur Pamplemousse was relieved to see the identikit picture bore only a superficial resemblance to himself, or at least the way he saw himself. Far be it for him to say so, but any self-respecting judge would have sentenced the man depicted in the made-up picture to five years' hard on sight. Even so, he didn't doubt the phone would start ringing at the Quai des Orfèvres once the likeness was circulated. It always did.

The drawing of Pommes Frites was inset into a square at the bottom of the page. Apart from having four feet and a tail, it was like no dog he had ever seen before. It wasn't altogether surprising that Jacques hadn't made the connection as yet, although that was perhaps only a matter of time. The people who had furnished the original description probably hadn't seen it either. Corrections would be made. Who knew what strange mutation they would end up with?

Jacques looked up. 'Any idea what the motive could have been?'

Monsieur Pamplemousse raised his hands to Heaven in a gesture of mute ignorance.

'Do you have the negative?'

'No problem.' Monsieur Pamplemousse looked inside the envelope. They were neatly packaged in a transparent envelope. 'I'll let you have it before you go.' The lab wouldn't thank him if he got truffled fingerprints all over it.

Jacques took another look at the print. 'It's not much to go on. It might be anyone in a crowd.'

'You could add height around 167 cm. Weight approximately 60 kilograms. Natty dresser. Dark suit – old-fashioned style. Expensive haircut. Manicured nails...'

'What is he? Some kind of gigolo?'

'*Non*.' Monsieur Pamplemousse shook his head. 'Anything but. I would say he's simply someone who spends a lot of time sitting in a barber's chair watching the world go by.'

'The dark glasses don't help. If he's got any sense he'll give up wearing them for a while.'

'I'm sure he already has.' Monsieur Pamplemousse took the opportunity to pour some more wine.

'You mean – the ones on the track? Bausch & Lomb?'

Monsieur Pamplemousse nodded. 'He is also left-handed.'

Jacques glanced up. 'You seem to know a lot about him.'

'That's about it. Except, I happen to know he is still around.'

'You've seen him since?'

'Outside the block – just after we talked on the phone.'

'Why on earth didn't you tell me?'

'Because . . .' Monsieur Pamplemousse shrugged. He was rapidly reaching the point where any further explanations might become difficult, not to say embarrassing.

'So what happened?'

Monsieur Pamplemousse launched into a brief run-down of the journey back from Rome with the Director's *petite cousine* and his return visit to the Gare de Lyon. In part, it helped crystallise his own thoughts and get them into perspective.

Not unexpectedly, Jacques wasn't slow to spot the deliberate mistake.

'Why did I go back there?' Monsieur Pamplemousse repeated the question, playing for time.

'You heard me. Don't tell me you've taken up train-spotting in your old age!'

'I mislaid something.' Even to his ears it sounded lame.

'The office of the Service des Objets Trouvés is in the main building,' said Jacques, 'not on *quai* "J". Come off it.'

'All right,' growled Monsieur Pamplemousse. 'Some-*one*.'

Jacques stared at him. 'Don't tell me! Not the girl you were supposed to be looking after?'

Monsieur Pamplemousse pushed the pictures of Caterina across the table. 'That's her.'

'Did you take these?' Jacques let out another whistle, longer this time, a mixture of surprise, envy and admiration. 'I thought you said she was still at school.' He tapped his teeth with the end of a pen. It had, recalled Monsieur Pamplemousse, been a source of irritation in the old days.

'So she is.' Sorting through the pile he found the one of Caterina arriving with the two nuns.

'Talk about before and after.' Jacques gave the second photograph a cursory glance and then returned to the pictures taken on the train.

'I'm surprised at you. Losing someone like that doesn't come under the heading of being careless – it's downright criminal; a chargeable offence. If you let me have the negs along with the other I'll get some more prints done straight away.'

Monsieur Pamplemousse shook his head. 'I'm afraid that is not possible.'

'Never mind. I'll get copies made of these. The sooner they're circulated the better.'

'You misunderstand me. When I said it is not possible, I meant simply that. I cannot let you have either the photographs or the negatives. They may fall into the wrong hands.'

'Fall into the wrong hands?' Jacques stared at him. 'You realise what you're saying?'

'I have made a promise that I would not tell the police,' said Monsieur Pamplemousse. 'At least, not for the time being.'

'A promise to whom? The family?'

'You could say that.' Monsieur Pamplemousse refused to let himself be drawn. 'You will have to accept my word that there are very good reasons.'

'Blackmail? Someone demanding a ransom? You know as well as I do we've got ways of dealing with that kind of thing. You only have to say the word.'

Monsieur Pamplemousse shook his head.

'Vice? Porno movies? Is that why you were asking all those questions earlier on?'

'If you start by thinking the worst,' said Monsieur Pamplemousse, 'anything else has to be better.'

'True. Well, I'll tell you something. If it has got anything to do with any of that and someone has got hold of her, they're not going to let go in a hurry. Anyway, what makes you think along those lines?'

'She is young, pretty, ambitious. She wants to be a model. She made it clear to me that she wishes to escape from her present life.'

'You mean she may have met up with someone like Madame Claude. Remember her?'

Monsieur Pamplemousse certainly did. In the 1970s Madame Claude had run one of the most fashionable and successful brothels of all time. Heads of state, royalty, millionaires, were said to have paid anything up to 10,000 francs a time for a one-night stand with the 'companion' of their choice.

'There could be worse fates,' said Jacques. 'If you recall, she chose the girls well – mostly out-of-work dancers or models. And she looked after them – bought their clothes, supervised their make-up, their hair, their lingerie, educated them, arranged for plastic surgery where necessary. Considering the number who went on to marry well, they couldn't really grumble. It was better than going to a finishing school as far as most of them were concerned. Every time you open one of the glossy *journaux* there they are, staring out at you.'

'That is hardly the point,' said Monsieur Pamplemousse. 'I agree there might be worse fates, but I would still be held responsible.'

'How about her parents? Have they been told?'

'I was hoping that wouldn't be necessary.' Monsieur Pamplemousse hastily tried to change the subject. 'Are there any Madame Claudes around these days?'

'There will always be Madame Claudes,' said Jacques. 'At 25 per cent commission off the top it wasn't bad going while it lasted. In the end, if you remember, the tax collector presented her with a bill of Fr.10,000,000 and she fled to America where she opened up a cake shop. When that failed she tried to make a come-back, but Martine Monteuil got her. Good old Martine.'

'The Brigade for the Repression of Pimping strikes again.'

'Who says she was pimping? Most of the girls were only too pleased to be working for her. At least it's not like it was in the old days. Remember the Corsicans just after the war? If any of the girls played up rough they used to rub coarse sugar into their faces. It played havoc with the make-up before it festered. Nowadays pimps are more discreet. They realise the value of not despoiling the goose that lays the golden eggs; they make sure any major disfigurement takes place where it isn't likely to be seen until it's too late.'

Monsieur Pamplemousse began to wonder if he had done the right thing in asking for Jacques' advice.

'So the answer to my question is no, you don't know of anything similar going on?'

'Not that I've heard of. Mind you, that doesn't mean to say it doesn't exist. Discretion is the name of the game in that kind of operation. Half the government would be out of a job if it weren't. Heads would roll. If you like I'll put out some feelers when I get back to the office. Give you a ring.'

'*Merci.*'

Jacques took one last look at the photographs of Caterina before returning them. 'And you think the man who was responsible for the murder at the Gare de Lyon – *if* he was responsible – has something to do with this girl's disappearance?'

'I think she was desperately trying to avoid him, put it that way.'

'So, if we find our man he may in turn lead you to the girl.'

'Exactly.'

'A real game of cat and mouse.' Jacques went back to the original photograph. 'It makes a change from *cherchez la femme* – although I know which I'd rather do. Care to swap?'

Monsieur Pamplemousse shook his head. He didn't feel much like joking.

'I don't blame you,' said Jacques. 'It isn't a lot to go on. Dark glasses work both ways. They may act as a good cover-up, but they also attract attention. What did he look like without them?'

'Thin-faced. A bit of a Charles Aznavour look-alike. I didn't get that close a view.'

'That's something, anyway.' Jacques took out his notebook.

'How about fingerprints?' asked Monsieur Pample-mousse. 'Anything on the glasses?'

'Fat chance. The frames were too thin.'

'Weapon?'

'He would have held the crown in the ball of his hand. Anything on the business end would have been wiped off when it penetrated.'

'How about trying another source?'

Jacques gave a deep sigh. 'Another source!' he repeated. 'What other source? Where? Are you holding out on me, Aristide?'

'Earlier this evening,' said Monsieur Pamplemousse, 'I received a telephone call. A hang up. If it was who I think it was, it must have been made from a call-box somewhere near here. I could hear an engine ticking over – it could have been a number 80 *autobus* waiting at the lights. They have a particular sound to them. In which case I suggest it might be worth checking the phones in the boxes down by the Place Constant Pecqueur . . . there's a group of three on this side of the road – nearly opposite the steps leading up from the Lamarck-Culaincourt Metro . . .'

Without waiting for him to finish Jacques reached for the phone.

While he was talking, Monsieur Pamplemousse cleared away the dishes and looked in the refrigerator to see what there was in the way of cheese.

He unwrapped a small wheel of Coulommiers and a wedge of Roquefort, still half-covered in its silver foil, and put them both on to a plate. There were two strawberry *barquettes*. Doucette must be psychic.

If he wasn't careful Jacques would start asking some awkward questions. Or, worse still, others would start asking Jacques awkward questions, and then the fat would really be in the fire.

Pommes Frites loitered in the doorway looking hopeful. It was long past his usual dinner time. Monsieur Pamplemousse obliged with a bowlful of biscuits and the remains of some stew he found in a plastic container. Then he returned to the other room.

Jacques looked up. 'They're on their way.'

The Coulommiers had a distinct Brie-like tang to it; the Roquefort felt firm and smooth as he unwrapped the foil. Monsieur Pamplemousse poured the last of the wine.

'It tastes of sheep.' Jacques pointed to the Roquefort. It was the kind of grudging back-handed compliment a man from the Rhône valley would pay to a cheese from another *département* of France. It didn't stop him cutting a second slice.

Having polished off the cheese and drained his glass, he disposed of a *barquette* and then looked at his watch. 'I must go. Thanks to you, I've got work to do.'

'I'll come down with you – I could do with some fresh air.' Monsieur Pamplemousse took Pommes Frites' lead down from its hook and ushered Jacques out into the hall.

Instinctively leaving the light on, he double-locked the door behind him.

The lift was still where Jacques had left it. Half the occupants in the block had probably gone away for the weekend, the rest were most likely eating out and wouldn't be back until late. It was always the same on a Friday night. A feeling of loneliness swept over Monsieur Pamplemousse as the enormity of the task ahead of him struck home.

Pommes Frites automatically stationed himself just inside the lift, breaking the ray of light to stop the doors closing before his master arrived.

'Look,' said Jacques, as Monsieur Pamplemousse joined him. 'I'll see what I can do – no questions asked. But I can't promise a lot. The old grapevine is in need of a bit of a watering at the moment. It's like I said earlier – cleaning things up is all very well, but it's really a case of sweeping the dirt under the carpet – it doesn't go away. In the meantime valuable sources of information have dried up. You'd probably do just as well putting out some feelers in the right quarters yourself.'

'*Merci.*' Jacques' words only served to underline Monsieur Pamplemousse's current mood.

As they made their way through the main hall on the ground floor, he glanced through the perspex front of his mailbox. He hadn't bothered clearing it when he arrived back earlier in the day and it looked full.

No doubt it was the usual collection of junk; he could list most of it by heart. A selection of cards from various organisations giving numbers to ring in an emergency – everything from a leaking washing-machine to lost keys. Boucheries Roger would be having yet another *promotion*. Halfway down the pile he spotted a copy of *Paris-Le Journal* – the free monthly guide to what was happening in the city. On the very top there was a large coloured brochure – most likely from the *super marché* in rue Marcadet. There would be nothing that couldn't wait.

'Thanks for the hospitality. I'll phone you tomorrow if I have any news.' Jacques slammed his car into reverse, executed a commendable half turn considering the width of the road, then roared off down rue Junot, tyres squealing as he took the bend, heading towards rue Caulaincourt and the telephone kiosks. As his tail lights disappeared from view Monsieur Pamplemousse heard a siren, then it faded away into the distance, deflected by the buildings, and everything went quiet.

The *parc* opposite his apartment was closed and he led the way down the road towards the steps leading down to rue Caulaincourt, pausing a couple of times on the way while Pommes Frites obeyed the call of nature.

If the worst came to the worst they would have to move elsewhere, of course. At least for the time being. Possibly, if he failed to find Caterina, it might mean leaving Paris for good. The Mafia never forgave – or forgot. Doucette would be heartbroken. So would he for that matter. Ambitions to become a member of the Boules de Montmartre team after he retired would remain unfulfilled.

Monsieur Pamplemousse decided against taking a short cut along the alleyway to his left which ran through to the back of the *parc*. It was narrow, with no escape routes on either side, and there was no point in taking unnecessary risks.

He stood for a moment at the top of the steps. Beyond the cobbled area at the bottom he could see a small crowd of spectators gathered round the kiosks – no doubt some of them were chafing at the bit because they wanted to make a call; most would have simply come to stare. There were a couple of squad cars parked nearby, their blue lights winking. The one facing the wrong way probably belonged to Jacques. A flash gun went off. They must be recording the fingerprints *in situ* as a precaution. Latent prints tended to go off quickly when the weather was cold. After that they would wait for the engineers to arrive in order to remove the actual phones so that they could work in comfort. Anyone who wanted to use them would be in for a long wait.

But if they left their apartment, where would they go? Would anywhere be safe? Despite the efforts of many, the Mafia still wielded a power which in many parts of the world reached into all corners of life. To be a Godfather was akin to being a feudal lord in ancient times. Their power was absolute. Upsetting them could provoke terminal arrangements.

Not wishing to get involved in the goings on in the *Place*, Monsieur Pamplemousse turned right and headed up the hill towards the Sacré-Coeur.

An occasional car drifted slowly past in the opposite direction, those at the wheel looking in vain for somewhere to park. At one point he took shelter in the narrow space between two vehicles as the last *Montmartrobus* of the evening swept down the hill towards him, the lights from its windows casting strange shadows on the ivy covered stone wall to his right. It was almost empty.

As the bus disappeared round a corner at the bottom, Monsieur Pamplemousse took the precaution of moving out into the middle of the road. He had read somewhere that in Italy there was a Mafia murder every ten hours. In America it was probably a lot more. In France? He had no wish to become a statistic in someone's crime report.

Pommes Frites had no such qualms. Glad to be out after being cooped up all the evening, he ran on ahead, reporting back every so often that all was well.

Monsieur Pamplemousse's thoughts went back to the murder at the Gare de Lyon. Had he just happened on it? He couldn't rid himself of the feeling that for some reason or other he might have been a direct cause.

The conductor was the only person able to shed any light on the subject; possibly the only one apart from himself able to identify the man on the train. If the news of Caterina's disappearance did leak out he would have been one of the first to be questioned. Better to eliminate any problems before they occurred. The very fact of Monsieur Pamplemousse returning to question the man must have been bad news.

But why had the murderer followed him back there? Monsieur Pamplemousse had a sudden thought. Supposing the reverse were true. Supposing the man – and his accomplice, whoever he was, were hoping *he* would lead them to Caterina. They must know by now that he had no idea where she was either? If that were the case, then for the time being at least, he would be safe. It was a Catch-22 situation and no mistake. If the news reached Sicily that Caterina was missing his number would be up. If he found her the same might apply.

The Place de Tertre was, as always, alive with tourists: noisy, colourful, like the setting from an operetta. Tables spilled out on to terrace and pavement alike; others filled the middle of the square. Surrounding it, artists' easels supporting ubiquitous pictures of wide-eyed street urchins, or cartoon dogs relieving themselves on walls and lamp-posts to the delight of their colleagues, vied for space alongside others depicting the surrounding land-marks. People sat under acetylene lights having their likeness sketched in charcoal or their silhouette cut out in black paper. Music in the French idiom gushed forth from dimly lit restaurants. Waiters in their white aprons bustled to and fro serving those hardy enough to dine outside beneath the trees.

Squeezing past a *commis* waiter carrying an ice-bucket in one hand and balancing a heavily laden tray with the other, Monsieur Pamplemousse was reminded for some unaccountable reason of a trick question his old school mistress, Mademoiselle Antoinette, was fond of asking new pupils: 'Which freezes first, a bowl of boiling water or a bowl of cold water?'

Very few ever got it right. Most newcomers automatic-ally plumped for what seemed the obvious answer; the bowl of cold water. They did so on the grounds that it 'stood to reason, of course'. The old hands looked superior as they grinned at each other.

He could still see the triumphant gleam in the mistress's eye as she pointed out there was no 'of course' about it, and that in life, 'reason' often flew out of the window.

'What reason? Where?' she would say, looking under her chair.

The explanation was simple enough. Under most circumstances the bowl of boiling water will turn to ice first. Why? Because it will give off steam and some of the water will evaporate, so that in the end there will be a smaller volume of water left to freeze.

Monsieur Pamplemousse carried on with the rest of his walk in an even more thoughtful mood than he had when he started. There was something odd about what was happening; something which didn't quite gel. Was it possible that he, too, was guilty somewhere along the line of letting reason fly out of the window?

The cobbled street was slippery after the rain, and he kept to the path, pausing every now and then to let a car go past. One way and another he wasn't sorry to get back to the Place Marcel Aymé.

If Il Blobbo was still watching the block, he was nowhere in sight. Monsieur Pamplemousse reached for his keys as he entered.

He hesitated as he passed the mail-box, and as he did so he noticed a small, white card on top of the pile. It hadn't been there when he went out, of that he was certain.

Opening the door, he reached inside and removed a plain postcard. It had his name on it, written in black ink – no address. It must have been slipped into the box while they were out. He turned the card over.

On the back someone had drawn a crude picture of a coffin.

6

THE OLDEST PROFESSION

'Pamplemousse! I fear I have bad news. I did not sleep at all well last night . . .'

Monsieur Pamplemousse stared at the telephone receiver in disbelief. Was it possible? Had the Director really woken him up simply to announce that he hadn't had his full quota of rest? Was there no limit to the chief's self-centredness? Indignation welled up inside him. Responses had to be choked back for fear he might say something he would afterwards regret.

He looked at his bedside clock and then relented slightly. It was almost nine-thirty. He must have slept like a log. Although it wasn't altogether surprising after all that had happened the day before, such a thing hadn't happened in years. Doucette must be wondering why he hadn't phoned.

Controlling his emotions with difficulty, Monsieur Pamplemousse held his fire in order to allow Monsieur Leclercq time to continue with a resumé of cause and effect. He hadn't long to wait.

'There is worse to come, Pamplemousse.'

'Worse, *monsieur*?' Monsieur Pamplemousse made a half-hearted attempt to keep the sarcasm from his voice. 'The hot water was running slightly cold, *peut-être*? Your morning *croissant* was perhaps not quite as fresh as it might have been? The *jus d'orange* a trifle acid?'

A hissing sound indicated that the Director was using his car telephone, so any immediate response was obliterated. As the car emerged from the other side of the tunnel or whatever else it was that had conspired to interrupt their conversation, it became apparent that he was on to another tack, and from his dolorous tones it was clearly one which was causing him considerable alarm.

'. . . pened this morning, Aristide. I received a postcard through the mail . . .'

Monsieur Pamplemousse experienced a momentary pang of conscience. 'Not bad news from Madame Leclercq, I trust?'

'No, Pamplemousse. Much, much worse. The message was in graphic form. The card bore a simple motif; that of a *bière*. A black *bière*!'

'A coffin?' Suddenly all ears, Monsieur Pamplemousse struggled into a sitting position. This was indeed bad news. He tried to strike a cheerful note. 'Perhaps it was a local *entrepreneur* mortician in Viroflay seeking extra business, *Monsieur*? Times are hard.'

'Times are never hard in the funeral business, Pamplemousse,' said the Director gloomily. 'Certainly not as far as the Mafia are concerned. In Italy they make sure business is booming.'

'But this is France, *Monsieur*.'

The Director was not to be consoled. 'If it is a genuine offer of service,' he continued, 'why did the company not append their name and address? Besides it had been hastily drawn by someone using a felt-tipped pen. No, I detect the hand of the Cosa Nostra. It is part of their tradition. They always warn their intended victim so that he knows exactly where he stands – or falls – and meets his death fully aware of who is responsible. It is what is known as "job satisfaction". Otherwise, when their victims are hit in the back by a bullet, they may die thinking it is only a passing sportsman with an unsteady aim.'

'But why you, *Monsieur*? You said yourself that if anything happened to Caterina the blame would fall squarely on my shoulders.'

'That was Thursday, Aristide. Since then I, too, have burned my boats. Yesterday evening Chantal's Uncle Caputo telephoned to ask after his daughter. On the spur of the moment I concocted a story about her arrival and all the things we have done together. First the Eiffel Tower, then the Musée d'Orsay, followed by a trip on a *bateau mouche* and hot *chocolat* at Angelina's. I must say, I became so fired with the whole thing I almost began to believe it myself. When he asked to speak to her I told him that she was tired out after all her exertions and that we had insisted on her going to bed early.'

'Was he not satisfied, *Monsieur*? It sounds perfectly reasonable to me.' Monsieur Pamplemousse seized the opportunity to climb out of bed and slip into his dressing gown.

'Unfortunately, Aristide, I then took a leaf out of your book. I pretended I was taking the telephone upstairs to her room. I think you would have been pleased with my efforts. I made great play with the fact that the guest room is on an upper floor and that due to the age of the building the second flight of stairs is unusually steep. Breathing heavily, I knocked on a nearby bureau to simulate the sound of tapping on a bedroom door. I then essayed the squeak of an unoiled hinge followed by a series of random snores to show how deeply Caterina was sleeping after her day out.'

Monsieur Pamplemousse held the receiver away from his ear as a sound like that of a wailing banshee emerged. His spirits fell on the Director's behalf. Knowing the chief's habit of going over the top once he had the bit between his teeth, it was more than possible that Uncle Caputo's suspicions had been roused.

'Was that it, *Monsieur*?'

'No, Pamplemousse, it was not.' The Director sounded shaken. 'It was another automobile coming in the opposite direction. I fear my concentration lapsed for a moment. As, indeed, it did yesterday evening.'

'What happened, *Monsieur*?'

'Flushed with success, I opened the window and imitated the mating call of a Mallard duck.'

'And?'

'The Mallard, Pamplemousse, is a *oiseau* which at this time of the year goes into eclipse. Neither duck nor drake is anywhere to be seen. Both are resting in the reeds. The male, having lost his flight quills – probably through having given way once too often to his carnal desires, is waiting for them to grow again. The female, exhausted by constant egg laying, remains at his side.'

Monsieur Pamplemousse resisted the temptation to ask if Uncle Caputo would be likely to know that fact. Clearly, the Director was in no mood for speculation.

'The die is cast, Aristide. I am now in it as deeply as your good self. There is only one consolation. There is a Sicilian saying: "*Uomo avvisato, mezzo salvato*" – a man who is warned is halfway to being saved. However, you can see why sleep eluded me, and why Caterina's early and safe recovery is of the essence . . .'

'Uncle Caputo can hardly have sent the card, *Monsieur*. He wouldn't have had time. I posted Doucette a card in Rome three days ago and that has yet to arrive.'

'Paris is but a telephone call away, Pamplemousse. Doubtless the Cosa Nostra have reciprocal mailing arrangements with their opposite number in France. The Mafia is organised on military lines. Each Godfather is like a general – responsible for his own territory. However, they have watertight methods of communication; their own codes.'

'But . . .'

'But what, Pamplemousse?'

'It doesn't make sense, *Monsieur*. Even if Uncle Caputo found your performance less than convincing, something else must have happened to arouse his suspicions. What could it have been?'

'I cannot answer that question, Pamplemousse. All I know is that the Mafia moves swiftly. Decisions are always instant and to the point. There is no dithering.'

'Unless . . .'

'Unless what, Pamplemousse?'

'Nothing, *Monsieur* . . .'

'Well, Pamplemousse,' said the Director severely, 'I trust that your deliberations on nothingness bear fruit within the very near future. Otherwise, I fear for both our lives ... not to mention the lives of our nearest and dearest.'

Monsieur Pamplemousse was saved any further interrogation as the Director's voice was engulfed by a wave of static. He waited a moment or two in case reception improved, then replaced the receiver and made his way towards the bathroom.

The news that the Director had also received a card bearing a picture of a coffin came as something of a surprise. Instinct told him that no matter how efficient the Mafia's lines of communication were, it could hardly have been sent by Uncle Caputo, or even at his instigation. But if Uncle Caputo hadn't sent it, who else would have done? And why? It would have to be someone who knew Caterina was missing. It would also need to be someone who was armed with a lot of information; the Director's home address outside Paris for a start – unless, of course, he had been followed too, but that suggested a whole army of people on instant call.

Lying back in the bath, Monsieur Pamplemousse's thoughts returned to events at the Gare de Lyon. The man on the Palatino had certainly been met by someone when he arrived in Paris – either that, or the two had travelled up separately on the same train. But if it went beyond that, if there were a number of other people involved, why had Il Blobbo turned up outside his apartment block the night before? Why hadn't someone else been given the job? It would have made more sense.

Pommes Frites, who looked as though he had been up

for some while, came out from under the table as his master entered the kitchen.

Monsieur Pamplemousse returned his greeting absent-mindedly as he put some coffee on to brew, then he sliced the remains of the previous day's *baguette* and put it in the toaster while he made himself a glass of fresh orange juice.

He should have asked the Director if his postcard had borne a stamp, or whether, like his own, it had been slipped in by someone amongst the rest of the mail.

Worries about Caterina, already tempered with fears about his own and Doucette's future, now included anxiety on the Director's behalf.

He gazed out of the kitchen window. At this time of the day, before the tour buses arrived, Montmartre was a haven of peace and quiet, much as it had been when Utrillo was alive and committed so much of it to canvas. In their time, Toulouse-Lautrec, Degas and Renoir had been inspired by their surroundings, too.

The storm had passed and the water he could see glistening in the sunshine as it ran down the gutters carrying all before it, came from underground pumps, not from the sky, which was blue and cloudless. Pigeons and sparrows carried out their morning ablutions. A few early-morning photographers were out and about.

'You had better make the most of it!' As he poured himself some coffee, Monsieur Pamplemousse couldn't help but wonder how much longer he and Doucette would be there to enjoy the view.

The apartment had become theirs soon after they were married. It was at a time when prices were low and they had just come into a little money after Doucette's father died. Such good fortune wouldn't happen twice. Marcel Aymé, the writer, was living there when they first moved in. They had seen him many times. A statue fashioned after a character from one of his books – *Le Passe-Muraille* – about a man who discovered he could walk through walls, had been made part of a real wall outside the building, and the *Place* itself had been named after him. The composer and conductor, Inchelbrect, had been another neighbour.

A smell of burning brought Monsieur Pamplemousse back to earth. He pressed a button to switch off the toaster, then buttered the slices and gave one to Pommes Frites while he consumed the rest standing up.

They could, of course, stay with friends for a while. He had lain awake the night before, going through various possibilities in his mind, rejecting them one by one. In the end he could only think of Doucette's sister in Melun. The thought depressed him. Anyway, he told himself it wouldn't be fair to involve anyone else.

One thing was very certain. They wouldn't be going anywhere at all unless he did something and did it quickly.

Pouring a second cup of coffee, he went into the living-room and picked up a copy of *Le Guide*. Flipping through the pages until he found the section he wanted, he reached for the telephone. It was early days, but it was worth a try. The Director wouldn't be able to hold Chantal's Uncle Caputo at bay for very long before the latter began to smell a rat, if he hadn't already.

On the principle that there was nothing like starting at the top, Monsieur Pamplemousse dialled the number for the first hotel listed under GRAND LUXE ET TRADITION and asked to be put through to the Concierge.

Using an assumed voice, for no reason he could logically have justified, he pretended to be telephoning on behalf of a very important foreign dignitary.

'I cannot mention his name. Discretion is paramount – you understand? He requires a suite and accommodation for his entourage...' Times were hard in the hotel business and there was no harm in holding out a carrot or two. 'He is also in need of someone to entertain him. A young lady of an amiable disposition.'

'When would this be for, *Monsieur*?' From the tone of the man's voice he might have been asking for an extra lump of sugar to be sent up to accompany his *café*.

'*Tout de suite*. He is arriving in Paris shortly and he is not a patient man. He will be wishing to relax after his long journey. He has a *penchant* for young Italian virgins...'

'*Puceaux Italiennes?*' It was the equivalent of two lumps.

'One would do,' said Monsieur Pamplemousse. 'Preferably convent educated and under seventeen, with dark hair. Money is no object. You know of an *agent* who could arrange for such things?'

The *concierge* lowered his voice. He knew of several likely candidates, but in his opinion they could all be sued under the trade descriptions act, particularly if *Monsieur*'s client spoke Italian.

'It stands to reason, *Monsieur*. It is a once-only situation. It is like a car – once it leaves the showroom it is second-hand. If the *Monsieur* you represent would care to lower his standards a little ... perhaps something with a low mileage on the clock?' The motoring metaphor had clearly been used before.

'My client is not accustomed to second best,' said Monsieur Pamplemousse severely. 'I would need to speak to your agent in person.'

No, that would not be possible. However, all things were open to negotiation . . . If *Monsieur* cared to make an appointment . . .

Monsieur Pamplemousse thanked the *concierge* for his trouble and hung up. He marked the entry in *Le Guide* with a cross. It might be worth bearing in mind for future reference.

At least the man had been honest, which was more than could be said for the next two.

'*Pas de problème, Monsieur,*' was the immediate response. They seemed surprised that he was bothering to ask, as though they had immediate access to an inexhaustible supply of young Italian virgins.

Lowering his sights slightly, Monsieur Pamplemousse set about tackling the HÔTELS GRAND CONFORT. The first on the list, a small but discreet establishment with an unusually high ratio of suites to rooms, sounded hopeful to begin with. After asking him to *attendez* for a moment, the person on the other end – he suspected it was the manager – had the call transferred to another line. He then asked Monsieur Pamplemousse if he would mind repeating his request in more specific terms. The man sounded slightly guarded, as though he were not the only one listening in to the conversation. Monsieur Pamplemousse put down the receiver.

It was not a promising beginning. It only served to underline the enormity of his task. In the old days he would have delegated it to a subordinate.

He flipped through *Le Guide* again. Some twenty or so

pages of hotels were listed. It would require a whole team of helpers on the job.

He wondered about giving the office a call – Loudier was an expert on Paris – he might have some ideas. Maybe he should have come clean with Jacques after all and told him the whole story. The trouble was it wouldn't stop there, and then the fat would really be in the fire and no mistake.

The phone rang. He reached for the receiver. Talk of the devil!

'I've been trying to get you for the last ten minutes!' Jacques sounded put out, as people always did when the person they wanted to speak to was engaged.

'Our man's put in an appearance.'

The proprietorial use of the word 'our' didn't escape Monsieur Pamplemousse's notice.

'You won't believe this, but he went into a security shop soon after nine o'clock this morning and bought up their entire stock of solar-powered security lights – the sort that switch on automatically if anyone comes within range of the infra-red beam.'

'How on earth did you get to know that?'

'It's run by someone who used to be in the Department – probably after your time – name of Frèche – *Crème Frèche* we used to call him. Anyway, he got fed up with advising people about what to do *after* they'd been broken in to. He was for ever putting business into the hands of other people and not getting any thanks for his trouble, so he handed in his badge and set up on his own account.'

'Why did he tell you?' asked Monsieur Pamplemousse.

'Because . . . and here's the funny part . . . it was a case of the biter bit. The man left without paying. You know what he said?'

'Tell me.'

'He wasn't into buying retail.'

Monsieur Pamplemousse couldn't help laughing. It wasn't funny, but . . .

'He simply admired the windows,' continued Jacques. 'Said what a pity it would be if they got broken, glass being expensive, and the cost of replacement being what it is these days. Also it wouldn't look good in a shop specialising in security. To have it happen more than once might well result in a great loss of trade. Then they walked out with all twelve units. Imagine!'

'They?'

'There was another man with him. Short. Stocky. Swarthy looking. Frèche felt he knew him from somewhere.'

'And you're sure the first man was the one I told you about?'

'A blow-up of your photo is on its way to Frèche right now, but the description fits. Besides, he spoke with an Italian accent. They both did.'

'What on earth would they want with twelve solar-powered burglar alarms?'

'Who knows? Unless it's for something entirely unconnected with the present problem. I asked Frèche and he came up with the suggestion that they might be using them to trigger off some kind of explosion. Apparently he's seen the idea written up in an American magazine. Rather a nifty thought. It doesn't require much imagination to think what would happen if you replaced the light with an ignition device and some semtex. The beauty of it is that being solar-powered you wouldn't need any external wiring.'

Monsieur Pamplemousse considered the proposition for a moment, but he couldn't for the life of him see where it might lead to.

'How about the telephone kiosk?' he asked. 'Any luck there?'

'Ah ... that's something else again. The fingerprint boys are still working on that. But thanks to you, they've struck a rich seam. Two breaking and enterings. Three sex offenders. A known heavy-breather. One with a record for armed robbery as long as your arm – or, to put it another way, by rights he *should* have a record as long as your arm, but apart from a spell inside for attempted murder we've never been able to pin anything on him. We should try it more often.'

'No other leads?'

'Give us a chance – it's not eleven o'clock yet.'

Monsieur Pamplemousse glanced at his watch. He had lost all track of time.

'Anything else I can do?' asked Jacques.

'Nothing ... No, wait ... Do you think you could ask around the local taxi companies? Allo Taxi operates around here. They're on 42-00-67-87, or there's G7 – they're on 47-39-33-33. See if they had a request from someone wanting to travel outside Paris late last night. South-west of the city – out towards Viroflay. If they don't turn up trumps you could try Taxis Bleus. After that I guess it's the car hire companies. They must have got some transport from somewhere. Unless, of course ...'

'Well?'

It occurred to Monsieur Pamplemousse that the second

man might have driven up from Italy.

'It could have a Rome number plate.'

'Thanks a heap!'

Despite his protest, Jacques was clearly beginning to enjoy the whole operation. 'I'm off to see Frèche. For two pins I'd set up in business myself. You know what they say – "If you can't beat 'em, join 'em". *Bonne chance.*'

'*Bonne chance!*'

Monsieur Pamplemousse sat for a moment or two sipping his coffee. Good luck was something he would need in abundance if he was to make any progress. Telephoning round the hotels had been something of a non-starter, but at least it had got his brain working. Perhaps it was time he did some field work – spread the word around a bit. A walk with Pommes Frites wouldn't come amiss. It would do them both good, and it would also be an opportunity to kill two birds with one stone; a chance to put plan 'B' into action.

It was very rare that he ventured on to the Boulevard Clichy these days, but unless things had drastically changed since his day, the 'girls' started early – especially the ones who could stand inspection by daylight – and even quite a few who couldn't.

From the top of the long flight of stone steps which ran down from the *Place* in front of the Sacré-Coeur he could see balloon sellers in the Square Willette far below; a splash of colour against the background of grey stone buildings. Behind him the tourists were out in force; the steps in front of the Sacré-Coeur itself were littered with them. He wondered if Il Blobbo was anywhere amongst them. Il Blobbo, or his friend. He certainly wasn't going to give them the satisfaction of looking.

In one of the streets off the Boulevard Clichy, just around the corner from the Moulin Rouge, he had his first encounter.

'*Un petit cadeau, Monsieur?*' Things hadn't changed. In the old days, when he had been in the force, it had always been a request for '*un petit cadeau*' – 'a little gift' – never a downright demand for money.

'I am looking for someone new . . .'

'Funny you should say that, dear.' The woman turned to a friend lounging inside a doorway and winked. 'It's my very first time out.'

'Someone . . . *very* new,' said Monsieur Pamplemousse politely. 'I mean *new* new.'

'You'll be lucky.' The welcoming smile disappeared.

'Who is looking after you? Is there someone I could talk to?' Monsieur Pamplemousse glanced through the doorway beyond the second woman towards a dimly lit flight of uncarpeted stairs. A smell of disinfectant, lust and disillusionment filled the air. There was the sound of running water from one of the upper floors; probably from a bidet.

'What's it to you?'

'It would be worth your while . . .' Monsieur Pamplemousse felt inside his jacket. 'I am doing an article . . .'

'Piss off,' said the second woman. '*Fiche le camp!* And take your dog with you. I've met your sort before.'

'Perhaps he could do with a quick *passe*?' said the first one. 'Not stuck up like his master.' She reached down and gave Pommes Frites a pat. 'How about it, *chérie*?'

'Doesn't know a good offer when he sees one,' said the second woman, as Pommes Frites backed away, showing his teeth. Releasing him from his leash, Monsieur

Pamplemousse gave up the conversation and carried on up the hill. It wasn't a good start. The occupants of a *Montmartrobus* eyed him with interest as it went past. He hoped there was no-one travelling on it who knew him.

Biding his time while he tried to sum up the situation, Pommes Frites followed on behind at a discreet distance. Straining his ears, he managed to catch several key phrases which emerged during the few brief con versations his master had on the way.

Unfamiliar words like 'quickie' seemed to predominate, followed by gestures which he couldn't recall having come across on any of his training courses.

Much as he loved and respected his master, the thought crossed Pommes Frites' mind more than once that Monsieur Pamplemousse's tastes seemed to have slipped; plummeted was a word he might have used had it formed part of his vocabulary. Translated into his own terms, if the first two women were anything to go by, most of them didn't look as though they were worth more than a passing sniff, if that. Nor were they dressed in a style which would have met with Madame Pamplemousse's unqualified approval. Leather trousers, pink tights and jackets unzipped to the waist, didn't normally form part of her wardrobe.

On the other hand, having said that, his master seemed perfectly capable of resisting any temptations thrust in his way, even to the point of enduring coarse laughter and jibes which clearly related to his manhood. It was all very strange.

Seeing a large, ginger-haired woman dressed in thigh boots and not much else, who seemed to be making lunges with a whip at anyone who came within reach,

Pommes Frites moved out into the road. As he did so he became aware of a car moving slowly up the hill behind them. Its four occupants, three men and a woman, were all in uniform, and all – including the driver – were glued to the windows.

A group of four *péripatéciennes* standing in a doorway enjoying a quiet smoke saw it too and immediately froze.

Unaware of what was going on, Monsieur Pamplemousse tried to engage the women in conversation. His blandishments were unsuccessful. They might have been turned to stone for all the notice they took.

'Is this man annoying you?' He heard a voice behind him.

'You are aware of the word *drageur*, *Monsieur*?' A second voice joined in.

Monsieur Pamplemousse turned and stared at the officers. 'Are you accusing me of accosting women?' he protested.

'We have been watching you. It's a bit early in the day to be out "trawling" isn't it?'

'What's the matter?' asked the policewoman. 'Couldn't you sleep?'

'What if I couldn't?' demanded Monsieur Pamplemousse. 'That is no business of yours.'

'There have been complaints.'

'Who has complained? Where? You have witnesses?'

The group exchanged glances.

'Witnesses?' said one of the gendarmes. 'What's he talking about?'

'Don't get cross, *Monsieur*,' said the policewoman, ogling him. 'I go off men who get cross.'

Monsieur Pamplemousse glared at her. Resisting the

temptation to say that if she was the last person on earth she would be so lucky, he sought instead to encapsulate the words in a look of contempt as he blew her a kiss.

'Attempting to importune a policewoman,' said the leader. 'That is a serious offence.'

'Harassment of the opposite sex,' broke in a second. 'That is also an offence these days.'

'It seems to me,' said Monsieur Pamplemousse, 'that I am the one who is being harassed.'

The number three piped up. '*Monsieur* is also doubtless aware that it is against the law in Paris to take a dog out without a lead?'

'A law,' said Monsieur Pamplemousse, 'which is never enforced.'

'Never?' The officer in charge held out his hand. '*La carte d'identité, Monsieur. S'il vous plaît.*'

Monsieur Pamplemousse knew better than to argue. It wouldn't help matters that Pommes Frites had just been relieving his boredom by doing a *pipi* on the rear wheel of the police car. Circumstantial evidence, it was true, for he was now looking in a shop window as though such an act would never cross his mind in a million years. All the same, he could have chosen a better time and place.

He felt in his pocket. He had already caught a faint gleam of recognition in the officer's eyes. Once he saw the name on his card the game would be up. There would be nudges and winks. Cracks about his past record; the affair at the *Folies*; his enforced early retirement.

He was right.

'Pamplemousse!' The man's face lit up. 'Of course! Pamplemousse of the *Sûreté*.'

Monsieur Pamplemousse decided to take a chance.

'*Exactement!* He nodded meaningly towards the four women, who were still frozen in their original pose.

'Please pay my respects to Madame Commissaire Martine Monteuil. Tell her my report is almost complete. It will be on her desk shortly – always provided, of course, I do not receive too many interruptions.

'I take it she has not changed? As I remember her, she does not suffer fools gladly. The Vice Squad has not been the same since she arrived on the scene. I hope I can tell her how helpful you have been in assisting me in my researches. All four of you.'

It worked. Returning the salutes, Monsieur Pamplemousse called Pommes Frites to heel and made his way on up the hill with all possible speed. He wondered how long it would be before the others remembered that Madame Monteuil had arrived long after his retirement.

One thing was certain. He would have to give Montmartre a miss for the time being.

Perhaps it was time he put plan 'C' into action. What was it Jacques had said earlier? 'If you can't beat 'em, join 'em.' It would be his last chance to make direct contact with those in the know.

But it would have to be later, after dark, when there was less chance of being recognised. The one thing he couldn't risk at the moment was being arrested. That would put an end to all his plans.

And it would have to be without Pommes Frites. Regrettably, they must not been seen together again for a while. From now on he would be on his own.

Quite how or when or why he had hit on plan 'C' was not a question uppermost in Monsieur Pamplemousse's mind as he parked his car near the Boulevard St Denis soon after dark that evening. Later on it would be, and later on, as it happened, wasn't as far away as he anticipated.

As he made his way towards that part of the Boulevard St Denis which lies to the south of the métro station, or as purists might have it, the point which marks the old city limits, indicated by the fact that beyond it the rue St Denis becomes the rue Faubourg St Denis – *faubourg* meaning 'suburb' – he had to confess to a feeling of excitement; the particular kind of excitement that can only come from doing a naughty deed after dark in a naughty world.

It was a feeling which grew with every step he took. Naughtiness, dressed in its party clothes, was lurking in every shop doorway and on every street corner. Not that any of it reached out to take him in its arms; rather the reverse, in fact. Shadowy figures drew back as they saw him approach.

It was a long time since Monsieur Pamplemousse had been in the area by day, let alone at night; still less on a Friday evening. As he remembered it, the bottom half – the end nearest the Seine – was mostly porno-movies and air-conditioned lesbian double acts. The top end was where all the action used to be, and by the sound of it things hadn't changed. There was a feeling of revelry in the air. He could hear whistles being blown. Shrill blasts rent the air, followed by cheers and counter cheers. It suited his purpose admirably. Any worries he might have had about attracting attention on his own account soon disappeared.

It was as he turned a corner into the rue St Denis that Monsieur Pamplemousse caught the full force of a fire hose on his chest. It knocked him sideways, propelling him inexorably into something which felt warm, soft, perfumed, and splendidly suited to cushion his fall. But his moment of respite was all too brief. Having taken stock of his sodden state, the owner of the *doudons* he was clasping uttered an apposite oath and sent him spinning on his way again.

From that moment on everything became a blur; a confused montage of black stockings and fish-net tights, of *gendarmes* with batons drawn, and of fighting, screaming girls in leotards, lace panties, leather, or simply total nakedness beneath fur coats thrown open to the elements.

Monsieur Pamplemousse also registered a group of strange hairy creatures in skirts, uttering wild barbaric shouts and grunts, the like of which he had never before encountered in the whole of his career.

At least it answered Jacques' question as to where the *travellos* had gone – from the Bois de Boulogne to the Boulevard St Denis.

Monsieur Pamplemousse was in the act of bending down to tie up his shoe-lace while he took stock of the situation, when he heard a guttural cry from somewhere near at hand. Before he had a chance to take evasive action, what felt like the claws of a small but powerful mechanical digger reached up from behind, groping as it came. As it made contact with his person it tightened its grip in no uncertain manner.

A cry of mingled rage, disgust and disappointment followed, but by then Monsieur Pamplemousse had all but passed out. He was vaguely aware of helping hands lifting him to his feet, half carrying him, half dragging him along the street, then he flew through the air and joined an assorted pile of other bodies in a van, where he lay gasping for breath like a stranded whale cast ashore after being caught in an Atlantic storm.

7

THE MORNING AFTER

Monsieur Pamplemousse woke to the harsh, metallic sound of a key turning in a lock and an iron gate being swung open. He felt cold, hungry and he had a splitting headache. He also perceived a dull ache in his private parts, which was hardly surprising considering what they had been through. He regretted now having left Pommes Frites at home. Pommes Frites would have stood up for him, administering punishment in like manner, but with compound interest. The unknown assailant who had grasped Monsieur Pamplemousse where it hurt most, would have felt the full measure of Pommes Frites' wrath encapsulated in molars which, in their time, had caused many an adversary to tremble in his boots. Nor would he have let go in a hurry.

Waving aside the token breakfast offering, Monsieur Pamplemousse asked once again to be allowed to use the telephone.

The request granted, he was led up a flight of stone stairs. His entry into the charge room was greeted by a cacophony of whistles and cat-calls from a large holding cage opposite the main desk. The population seemed to have swelled far beyond its maximum capacity level since he had last seen it. It was like a scene from the Snake Pit; Brueghel gone mad. Worse even, if that were possible, than the episode in the rue St Denis the night before; although at the time that had seemed bad enough.

Monsieur Pamplemousse gazed at the occupants of the cage, some barely able to stand, clutching the bars for support, others lying on the floor out for the count, their spreadeagled hairy legs protruding at odd angles from their skirts as though long since abandoned by their owners. In a far corner a small group were crouched over a communal bowl, their heads clutched in their hands.

He turned to the inspector behind the desk. It was someone he hadn't seen before. The early morning shift must have taken over. 'You have had a busy time.' It was a statement rather than a question and as such met with a non-committal grunt.

'Brazilians over here for the operation?' hazarded Monsieur Pamplemousse. '*Animaux*,' growled the officer. 'It is worse than the zoo. You are lucky you got here early and had a cell to yourself. Some of us had to sit here all night looking at them.' He shook his wrist in time-honoured fashion.

'So who are they? Where are they from? Don't tell me the "B" team from Mars are playing an away match?'

From the look on the man's face it felt as though he could be getting warm.

'*Les écossais*. Scotsmen. They are over for the Rugby International. It is the big match of the season today. With supporters like that who needs a ball?'

'Who, indeed?' Suddenly it all became clear. What a night to have picked! Monsieur Pamplemousse gazed round at them. 'They won't see the game.'

'*Non!*' The inspector could hardly conceal his pleasure at the thought as he handed Monsieur Pamplemousse the telephone. 'It is the same every year. They come – they get drunk – they miss the match – they go home again. Not that there is any doubt as to who will win. The matter is one of pure *formalité*.'

'If it is like that before the match, think what it will be like tonight!'

Monsieur Pamplemousse dialled the Director's home number for the umpteenth time and then stood back, half expecting to hear the engaged signal, as had happened the last half dozen or so times during the night when he had tried. He caught the eye of the inspector looking at him.

'Haven't I seen you before?'

'Possibly.' Monsieur Pamplemousse turned away. He had no wish to be quizzed on the subject of his past. Once word got around that old Pamplemousse of the *Sûreté* was in the nick he would never hear the last of it.

He received several blown kisses from the occupants of the cage for his pains.

'*Allo. Allo!* Is anybody there?' It sounded like a wrong number.

'*Pardon. Excusez-moi . . .*'

'Pamplemousse! Thank goodness it is you.' The voice suddenly became recognisable, as though a sock had been removed from the speaker's mouth.

'I have been trying to telephone you, *Monsieur*, but each time you were engaged . . .'

'Not engaged, Pamplemousse . . . in hiding! I took the

131

precaution of leaving the receiver off the hook in case there was another call from Sicily. Where have you been?' The Director contrived to make it sound as though the fault lay entirely with his subordinate.

'It is not so much where I have *been*, *Monsieur*, as where I still am. That is the reason why I have been trying to contact you.'

'You have news of Caterina?'

Monsieur Pamplemousse glanced round at the inspector, who was making play of filling in a report form. Clearly it wasn't receiving his undivided attention.

He cupped a hand over the mouthpiece. 'It is hard to say, *Monsieur*.'

'Why is that, Pamplemousse?' The Director's booming voice came through loud and clear. 'Are you not alone? Is someone else listening in to our conversation?'

As Monsieur Pamplemousse bent over the counter someone opened the door leading to the street and he felt a draught of cold air sweeping up behind him. It provoked another round of whistles, cat-calls and what were clearly, from the accompanying gestures through the bars, obscene Celtic remarks being directed at his nether regions from the occupants of the cage.

'Pamplemousse, what is that noise I hear?' barked the Director. 'It sounds like something out of *Grand Guignol*. Is someone being attacked?'

'It is nothing, *Monsieur*. It is simply that my frock has a large tear down the back ... I am being given the once-over by a group of Scotsmen who are the worse for drink ...'

'Did I hear you use the word frock, Pamplemousse?' The Director sounded in a state of shock.

'*Oui, Monsieur*. I can explain everything, but for the moment my hands are tied . . .'

'Give me your address,' barked the Director. 'If, indeed, you are in a fit state to know it. I will arrange for a dispatch rider to deliver you a knife as soon as possible . . .'

'*Monsieur*, I can explain.'

'There is no need to, Pamplemousse,' said the Director coldly. 'Provided it does not bring opprobrium on *Le Guide*, what you do in your spare time is no concern of mine, although I must confess there are times when your extra-mural bedroom activities leave me at a loss for words.

'Bondage is something I have never been able to understand. Neither is sado-masochism. I admire your tenacity in leaving no stone unturned when you are hot on the scent, but there are limits. I fail to see what you hope to gain by these esoteric avenues of investigation, other than to satisfy some bizarre twist in your character in the process.'

'*Monsieur*, I am telephoning you because I am in urgent need of some string-pulling . . .'

Monsieur Pamplemousse winced as a crack like a pistol shot nearly shattered his ear-drum. It sounded as though the Director might be striking his telephone on a particularly solid item of furniture. It said much for the makers that the handset still worked. If anything, the quality seemed to have improved.

'Things go from bad to worse, Pamplemousse. How dare you try and involve me in your sordid bedroom games! Were it not for the exceptionally good turn you have done me, I would be sorely tempted to leave you to stew in your own juice for a while. As it is, I will do what I can, but it will not be easy. Today is Saturday and most of my contacts in the higher echelons of authority will have left Paris for the weekend. However, before I do anything, I must come and see you in order to apprise myself at first hand of the salient facts . . .'

'That will not be necessary, *Monsieur*.' Monsieur Pamplemousse closed his ears to all around and spoke coldly and clearly into the telephone. 'The salient facts, as you call them, are quite simple. Firstly, I am not in the habit of indulging in bondage, or in sado-masochism. Nor, for that matter, are my hands tied to any bedposts. It was a metaphor I used on the spur of the moment in order to describe my present situation. I am in a *Gendarmerie* in the 2nd *arrondissement* and I am in urgent need of some string-pulling in order to secure my release. How I came to be here in the first place is something I will explain to you later, but for the time being every second spent arguing is a second wasted at a time when each and every one is precious. Secondly, either you wish me to continue with my task, or you do not.'

'Pamplemousse . . .'

'I am in à *gendarmerie* in the 2nd *arrondissement*,' repeated Monsieur Pamplemousse. 'A word in the ear of the examining magistrate, *peut-être*? Otherwise . . .'

'Aristide . . .'

Monsieur Pamplemousse replaced the receiver. He hesitated, wondering whether to try his luck and ask if he might be allowed an extra telephone call in order to get a message through to Jacques, but he decided against it. The desk officer was all ears. Word would spread like wildfire. Besides, the *gendarmerie* had enough problems on its hands without his adding to them.

As it happened Monsieur Pamplemousse had hardly got back to his cell, a matter of ten or fifteen minutes at the most – although it could have been more, he had lost all feeling for time since he had been deprived of his watch the night before – when he received another summons.

'You're in luck,' said a *gardien*, as he opened the cell door. 'You must have friends in high places. Someone has been talking to someone.'

Maddening though the Director could be at times, Monsieur Pamplemousse couldn't help but feel grateful for his 'connections'. On this occasion he really had excelled himself, breaking all previous records.

'Sign here.' The inspector gave Monsieur Pamplemousse an odd look as he spread an assortment of belongings across the counter.

Anxious to be on his way as quickly as possible, Monsieur Pamplemousse did as he was bidden and swept the articles into a large brown paper bag without even bothering to check them.

'Why?' The officer looked him up and down sadly, then shook his head. 'What possible reason?'

Monsieur Pamplemousse felt tempted to say that it had seemed like a good idea at the time, but he thought better of it. It was the kind of remark that was open to misinterpretation.

'It happens when there is a full moon,' he said. 'I can't help myself.' The simple explanations were often the best. At least they avoided a lot of tedious explanations.

'I've got an uncle like that.' A *gendarme* pecking away at an ancient typewriter near the back of the room looked up. 'About the same age as you. He can't help it either.'

'I could lend you a skirt if you like,' said a woman colleague.

'That will not be necessary,' said Monsieur Pamplemousse stiffly.

The inspector nodded towards the cage. 'It must be worse where that lot come from. Especially when there's a full moon.'

The walk back to his car was not a happy one for Monsieur Pamplemousse. The Boulevard de Bonne Nouvelle was crowded with people heading west to do their shopping, but at least his car was still astride the pedestrian crossing where he had left it.

He drove the rest of the way home crouching as low as he could behind the dashboard. From a distance there were times when it looked as though there was nobody at the wheel at all; a fact which didn't pass unnoticed by several alert members of the Paris police force, who duly reported the phenomenon.

Pommes Frites greeted his master in somewhat muted fashion; a mixture of relief at seeing him again, coupled with anxiety at what might befall him next; joy tempered with fear that he might be too late to rescue him from whatever fate had in store. Tail-wagging was sincere but tentative.

Seeing that his friend and mentor clearly had other things on his mind, Monsieur Pamplemousse put two and two together and led him to the lift, where he pressed the button for the ground floor. Pommes Frites was well able to look after himself when he got downstairs, but to make doubly sure Monsieur Pamplemousse rang the *concierge* to let him know he was on his way.

It wasn't until he went into the bathroom and caught

sight of his reflection in the mirror that he realised for the first time the full extent of the damage he had suffered. It was no wonder Pommes Frites had looked worried.

His make-up was, to put it mildly, no longer in pristine condition. Lipstick, eyeshadow and rouge had run in all directions, and the foundation cream had certainly not been improved by a night's growth of beard. His face bore a remarkable resemblance to an early map of the Camargue marshlands. As for Doucette's frock; it looked like something the cat had brought in.

Monsieur Pamplemousse lay in the bath for a long time, growing gloomier and gloomier as he took stock of the situation. He was rapidly running out of ideas, and he was no nearer finding Caterina than when he had started. Short of going against the Director's wishes and bringing in the authorities, he didn't know which way to turn. And if he did that, Heaven alone knew where it would all end. The fat would be in the fire and no mistake.

Half an hour later, dressed and ready to face the world again, he started going through his belongings to make sure everything was there. His Cross pen, his Cupillard Rième watch – both of which he would have been mortified to lose – were safe and sound. The contents of his wallet looked intact – he must have held on to Doucette's handbag like grim death during the fracas. Emptying the contents on to the dining-room table – keys, *télécarte* and various other odds and ends, he came across a small sealed envelope bearing his name. The flap was tightly sealed down and he had to slit it open with the tip of his pen. Inside, there was a card. It bore the name of an Italian restaurant called Mamma Mia's, in the 2nd *arrondissement*.

Someone had scrawled a message across the card: ASK FOR MARIA. Alongside it there was an arrow pointing towards the right-hand edge. He turned the card over. On the back the same hand had written the day's date and a time – '19.30'.

Monsieur Pamplemousse gazed at it for a moment. Somewhere in the back of his head the name Mamma Mia rang a faint bell.

He picked up his copy of *Le Guide* and thumbed through the Paris section devoted to the 2nd *arrondissement*, but there was no mention of the restaurant. It was hardly surprising. Checking the address again on a map, he saw it was in the north-eastern section – not very far, in fact, from where he had left his car the night before: hardly a fertile eating area.

He jumped as the phone rang.

'*Allo.*'

'Pamplemousse!' It was the Director.

'*Monsieur!* I cannot thank you enough.'

'There is no need. I have to admit straight away, your release had nothing whatsoever to do with any efforts on my behalf. In fact I telephoned the station where you were being held to let you know that it was as I feared – most of my contacts are out of Paris for the weekend and that it might take some time, when they informed me you had already left.'

'That is very strange, *Monsieur*.'

'Very,' said the Director drily. 'The inference was that someone on high has been leaned on. It certainly had nothing to do with me.'

Monsieur Pamplemousse absorbed the fact. If it wasn't the Director, who could it have possibly been?

'Regardless of who was responsible, Aristide, it is good news. I am sorry if I flew off the handle this morning – especially after the exceptionally good turn you did me. I have been thinking about it since then . . .' He broke off. 'Are you listening, Pamplemousse?'

'*Oui, Monsieur.*' Monsieur Pamplemousse sounded puzzled. 'It was something you said a moment ago . . . about my doing you a good turn . . . You used the word *exceptionelle.*'

'Modest as ever, Pamplemousse. You are a strange mixture and no mistake. One moment you indulge in practices which would bring a blush to a raven's cheeks, the next moment you hide your light under a bushel. I refer of course to your kind act in arranging for the overnight installation of what I can only call an early warning system. There are lights over every door. From where I am standing I can see at least three. I trust you will bill *Le Guide* direct . . . I will see to it that Madame Grante in Accounts gives it her approval . . . I must also ask you to pass on my thanks to the workmen. They must have worked swiftly and silently. I didn't hear a thing.'

'*Monsieur* . . .' Monsieur Pamplemousse tried hard to keep the note of alarm from his voice. 'Where are you speaking from?'

'I am on my way downstairs, Pamplemousse. I wish to carry out a closer inspection of your arrangements. So far I have only seen them from my bedroom window.'

'What is the weather like, *Monsieur*? Is the sky very blue?'

'It is indeed, Pamplemousse. The sun is almost over the tree tops. After all the rain, we are in for a perfect day. Spring is here at last.'

'*Monsieur*, you must not, under any circumstances, set foot outside your house until I have given the "all clear". Furthermore, you must warn anyone who approaches – the mailman – the gardener – not to come anywhere near . . .'

'Why in Heaven's name?' boomed the Director. 'I cannot be incarcerated in my own house like this, Pamplemousse. I have important work to do . . .'

'Because, *Monsieur*, the "arrangements" as you call them, have nothing whatsoever to do with me. Furthermore, I have good reason to believe the lights contain high explosive . . .'

'High explosive?' repeated the Director. 'Is this some kind of joke . . .'

'No, *Monsieur*. I assure you, it is deadly serious.'

During the silence which followed, Monsieur Pamplemousse took the opportunity to go through his wallet, checking the contents with his free hand.

'What shall I do, Aristide?'

'I can only suggest you pray for rain, *Monsieur*. I will try and obtain a copy of the instruction manual, but as the devices are solar-powered I fear it may need a long spell of inclement weather before the batteries lose their charge. I will also check with the weather bureau.

'At least you are safe from attack. The device will work both ways. Short of using a helicopter, not even the Mafia can get anywhere near.'

'That is true, Aristide.' The Director sounded slightly mollified. 'You know, I hadn't thought of that.'

'It is the Mob's favourite form of murder,' said Monsieur Pamplemousse. 'Remember the "pineapples" in the Twenties.'

'No, Pamplemousse, I do not remember the "pine-apples" in the Twenties. And I do wish you wouldn't keep using the word "murder". It makes me nervous.'

Monsieur Pamplemousse placed the receiver under his chin. While they were talking he had suddenly stumbled across an item he had completely forgotten about.

'Later, *Monsieur*,' he said. 'I will telephone you later.'

'Pamplemousse . . .'

Monsieur Pamplemousse replaced the receiver, then he picked up the piece of paper on which Caterina had written her forwarding address. It was the same as that for Mamma Mia's. He compared the handwriting with that on the card, but it was totally different.

The telephone rang again, but he ignored it. It was the first glimmer of a breakthrough and he wanted time to think. His mind was racing with possibilities, none of which seemed to make any kind of sense.

It was only then that he realised Pommes Frites still hadn't returned from his walk.

Monsieur Pamplemousse turned into the rue Jardis and drove slowly along it until he saw the address he was looking for. It was sandwiched between a store specialising in costume jewellery and another stacked to the ceiling with bales of dress material.

By day the whole area would be a seething mass of humanity, the pavements awash with men struggling to manipulate trolleys piled high with cardboard boxes; the traffic almost permanently grid-locked. It was a wonder any business got done at all. Now it was relatively quiet and peaceful.

The street was narrow and strictly one-way, with room

for parking on one side only; a rule enforced by iron posts set in the pavement. Having passed a vacant space almost opposite the restaurant, he managed to find another some 20 or so metres further along.

Backing in to it, Monsieur Pamplemousse switched off his lights and checked the time on his watch – nineteen-twenty. He hadn't been aware of another car on his tail, but seeing he was early it was worth waiting a few minutes, just to make doubly sure.

Mamma Mia's was in one of the less salubrious parts of the 2nd *arrondissement*; an area packed with sweat shops catering for the rag trade. In a game of Monopoly, landing on it would not under any circumstances have constituted a stroke of good fortune. Building a hotel on the site would have been an act of desperation on the part of the unlucky thrower of the dice. On the other hand, during the daytime it must enjoy a near monopoly in providing food for the workers – if they were allowed that much time off.

There were net curtains at the windows and the lights were on inside, but there was no sign of anyone either coming or going. The woodwork looked as though it could have done with a lick of paint, as indeed, could most of the other buildings round and about.

The few people abroad wore a furtive air, as though they spent their lives waiting for the tap on the shoulder. An old woman shuffled past pushing a pram. She stopped by a pile of garbage just beyond the restaurant and poked at it with a stick for a moment or two before going on her way, her hopes unfulfilled.

Monsieur Pamplemousse waited until the hands on his watch said exactly nineteen-thirty, then he climbed out of his car, locked the door and crossed over the street, wondering what to expect, but prepared for the worst.

To his surprise, the restaurant was almost full. In his experience Italians usually didn't begin eating until much later in the evening, whereas most of the occupants of Mamma Mia's looked as though they were already halfway through their meal.

As he closed the door a man he took to be the *patron* came forward to greet him.

'*Monsieur* has a reservation?'

'The name is Pamplemousse.'

The man's face lit up. 'Ah, *signore*. We are expecting you.' He led the way towards a row of three small tables placed in front of a *banquette* seat which ran along the fabric-covered wall of an alcove near the window. It faced the back of the small entrance lobby, so the whole area was relatively isolated from the rest of the room. Preparations had clearly been made for his arrival, for all three tables carried a *Reservé* sign and the chairs which normally would have faced the *banquette* had been removed.

Taking away the middle sign, the *patron* pulled the table out so that Monsieur Pamplemousse could seat himself.

'You are expecting others?'

The man shook his head. 'It is so that you will not be disturbed.' He put a finger to his lips. '*Molto tranquillo.*'

Suddenly realising how hungry he was, Monsieur Pamplemousse looked around as he settled down. Taste buds began to throb as he unfurled a napkin and tucked it inside his collar. The atmosphere felt warm and inviting. There were propitious signs everywhere. People were eating with obvious pleasure. From the kitchen there came the sound of a woman's voice singing an aria from *Madame Butterfly*. He wondered if it was Mamma Mia herself. A happy chef was a good chef.

On the matchboarded wall opposite him there was a large mirror decorated with an advertisement for Cinzano. Framed pictures of past customers and other memorabilia covered the wall on either side of it.

A bottle of Sicilian wine arrived on his table, along with a long glass containing some sticks of wrapped *grissini*.

'Tell me,' said Monsieur Pamplemousse. 'Who is Maria? Will she be joining me?'

'Later, *signore*.' The *patron* pointed towards the kitchen. 'For the moment she is busy. It is Saturday night. In the meantime she says you must eat and enjoy yourself.'

'She is your wife?'

'*Sì, signore*.' Monsieur Pamplemousse looked for the menu but the owner held up his hand in protest.

'*Signore*, for you, she is preparing *spaghetti all'acciuga in salsa d'arancia* – spaghetti with orange and anchovy sauce. It is all home made.' Lip-smacking was accompanied by the classic finger and thumb to the mouth gesture. '*Molto buono*.'

'Home made . . . on the premises?' In his experience 'home made' was often a euphemism for a superior brand of factory prepared food.

'*Signore!*' Reproach was evident in the *patron*'s eyes.

Monsieur Pamplemousse expressed sorrow that such a thought should have entered his mind.

'Then, tonight, we have *ossobuco*. It is served with *risotto*.'

'*Risotto milanese*? With saffron and Parmesan cheese?' The owner nodded with pleasure.

'And the *ossobuco* . . . it comes with the long thin spoon for extracting the very last of the bone marrow?'

'The "tax agent"? *Sì, signore.*'

Monsieur Pamplemousse beamed back at him. It was a genuine little corner of Italy and no mistake. He reached for his notebook, then thought better of it. He might need all his powers of concentration. No matter. Perhaps when it was all over he would pay the restaurant a return visit.

He was tempted to ask if the owner's wife was in any way related to Uncle Caputo. It was possible. If such were the case she might even know the Director's wife. That would explain why there was no mention of the establishment in *Le Guide*. The Director would fall over backwards rather than be accused of nepotism by any of his rivals.

'Maria will join you later . . .' The *patron* was about to leave when he suddenly broke off and stared towards the window, almost as though he had seen a ghost.

Following the direction of his gaze, Monsieur Pamplemousse felt his own heart miss a beat. Scarcely a metre away from him two faces were peering into the restaurant through a gap in the curtains. Even without the dark glasses one of them was clearly recognisable as the man on the train. His eyes were dark, steely grey and totally expressionless.

As they disappeared from view the owner crossed himself and hurried to the door, returning a moment later followed by the two men. As they headed towards Monsieur Pamplemousse's corner, he made a half-hearted attempt to bar their way.

· '*Signore*. The tables in the window are reserved.'

'*Grazie*.' The shorter of the two men pushed past him, picked up the two *Reservé* notices and tossed them on to the floor. An uneasy silence descended on the restaurant.

Il Blobbo, the long, thin one, seated himself on Monsieur Pamplemousse's right and spoke first.

'How are things in the funeral business?' he asked.

The short, fat one laughed as he seated himself on the other side. It was not a pleasant sound.

Glancing at his reflection in the mirror, Monsieur Pamplemousse saw only too well what was meant by the remark. He also caught sight of something silver sticking out of Il Blobbo's top pocket. It looked like the end of a hat pin.

Gradually the chatter in the main body of the room started up again, but as he sat very still, waiting for his *spaghetti all'acciuga* to arrive, Monsieur Pamplemousse realised that the singing in the kitchen had stopped.

8

IN THE SOUP

Monsieur Pamplemousse was still waiting for his first course some twenty minutes later. All he had to show for his pains was a plateful of crumbs and some screwed-up paper left over from the supply of *grissini*.

He made the final stick last as long as possible; which was more than could be said for the bottle of wine. It was one of the newer, lighter Sicilian blends, unclassified for lack of ancestry. Pleasant enough, but as the picture beneath the name suggested, it was meant to be quaffed along with the food of the region, not drunk purely and simply as an *apéritif*. Food of any region would have been a welcome bonus.

He eyed a symbolic loaf of the local bread which occupied a place of honour on the counter. It was shaped like a three-breasted woman. He wondered what would happen if he went across and broke one of them off to assuage his hunger. Would it cease to be a symbol of prosperity?

It was good to find a restaurateur who had pride in his

origins, but as time passed he couldn't help wondering if the connection went deeper than that. Perhaps not as a 'soldier' who had been through the ceremony and was on a percentage – he would need to have committed a murder for that, and he didn't look the type – but perhaps as an unpaid 'associate'; someone with a 'connection'. If that were the case he couldn't expect any help from that direction.

More than once Monsieur Pamplemousse tried to catch the owner's attention, but he was clearly avoiding that end of the room. As soon as there was the slightest sign of a hand being raised he rushed out into the kitchen. Once, Monsieur Pamplemousse saw what he took to be Mamma Mia herself staring straight at him through the hatch. It was hard to tell what she was thinking. Her expression was a mixture of frustration and consternation, and when he caught her eye she, too, crossed herself.

Shortly afterwards a small boy he took to be a member of the family emerged and passed through the restaurant. He returned a few minutes later armed with a large packet partly concealed beneath his jacket. It was impossible to see what was written on the side. Perhaps he had been out for his own supper?

Monsieur Pamplemousse's hunger pangs grew worse as he watched the others around him tuck in to their food. Mounds of pasta melted away before his gaze; plates were wiped clean with large chunks of bread. One party in a far corner of the room even had the gall to return a dish of *pollo ripieno alle noci* only half eaten. The walnut stuffing, according to the host, had overwhelmed the delicate taste of the chicken. Apologies were profuse.

They were allowed another choice and it arrived within minutes.

The men on either side of him had been served almost straight away by a young waitress; a comely, if taciturn girl, who apparently suffered badly from a disease common to her calling. Galloping myopia. She reached past Monsieur Pamplemousse as though he didn't exist.

The thin one, the one on the train – Il Blobbo, ate his bowl of *ravioli* slowly and with precision, savouring each and every mouthful as though he had all the time in the world. The short, fat one gobbled his down noisily, as though there were no tomorrow. Both methods were a form of torture.

Apart from their opening remark, neither had uttered a word during the whole time they had been there. The chill which had entered the establishment on their arrival gradually permeated the room, communicating itself from table to table like a slow-moving cloud of dry ice.

'Why are you here?' Monsieur Pamplemousse broke the silence.

'Because we are hungry.' Once again it was the thin one who spoke first.

'*Sì. Abbiamo molto fame.*' His companion showed a mouthful of pasta. A dribble of olive oil landed on his tie and began to spread.

'Does your friend always speak with his mouth full?' asked Monsieur Pamplemousse.

The first man allowed himself the ghost of a smile.

Monsieur Pamplemousse tried again. 'What have you done with the girl?'

Both men stopped eating and stared at him as though he had said something totally outrageous. He watched their reflection in the mirror as they exchanged a quick glance.

The fat one nudged the other. 'You know something? He's a joker. He could be flavour of the month.'

'You realise I could call for help.'

The man he had christened Il Blobbo reached for a bottle of Pellegrino. He poured the water slowly and carefully into his glass.

'But you won't.'

Something about the total arrogance of the man suddenly made Monsieur Pamplemousse's gorge rise.

'So, what is keeping you? Why don't you get on with it? Do you enjoy playing games?'

His outburst fell on stony ground. Neither man paid him the slightest attention. They just carried on eating.

Monsieur Pamplemousse went back to examining his empty wine bottle, wondering about the possibility of making a break for it. The thin one was right, of course. Hemmed in as he was between the two of them, he wouldn't get out from behind the table, let alone reach the door. It was a game of cat and mouse. He glanced around the restaurant. One thing was certain. He wouldn't receive much help from the other occupants either. And why should he expect any? They were mostly locals, out for a quiet night with their family. They wouldn't want to be involved.

Perhaps it was a case of being wise after the event, or accepting what should have been obvious from the start, but seeing the two men together at close quarters, they both had their origins written all over them. Hoodlums in black suits. It was a sort of uniform, the kind of clothing other people kept for weddings and funerals:

almost like a badge of office. The Mafia was nothing if not conservative.

But if what the Director had said were true – that there was nothing more dishonourable for a member of the Cosa Nostra than to be involved in prostitution – and his own limited experience confirmed the fact, then what were they up to? Why were they in Paris?

Their arrogance came naturally to them, but was it not overlaid with something else? Once again, he found himself searching for the right word. Unease? Fear? Despite their outward show of indifference, they were definitely on edge about something. The fat one's nails were bitten almost to the quick. Monsieur Pamplemousse decided to have another go.

'Don't tell me you have no idea where the girl is either? Is that why you have been following me?'

It was number two's turn to speak first. He looked at his partner and winked.

'No flies on his nose, eh?'

The thought made him laugh so much he nearly choked. It gave Monsieur Pamplemousse no small pleasure to see the man's tie land in his pasta.

He decided that perhaps the best thing to do was sit back and see what happened. If he waited long enough he might even get served.

'*Encore!*' Seeing the waitress approaching his side of the room, Monsieur Pamplemousse pointed to the bottle.

Settling back in his seat again, he happened to glance towards the window and as he did so he caught a momentary glimpse of something black and wet pressed against the outside of the glass. It took all his self-control not to register the fact. At first sight it looked not unlike one of the truffles he had brought back from Italy; a *tuber melanosporum* from Périgord, rather than the Piedmont variety, but there the resemblance ended.

It struck Monsieur Pamplemousse that Pommes Frites – for there was no doubt in his mind as to the ownership of what at second glance was clearly a nose – wore his enigmatic expression. Their eyes met for a fraction of a second and there wasn't the faintest flicker of recognition. The fact didn't bother him unduly, for he knew Pommes Frites was too well trained to give the game away. All the same, it would have been nice to have some reaction. A reassuring bang on the restaurant door with a paw perhaps, or even a faint howl of sympathy from further along the street wouldn't have come amiss in the circumstances.

But Monsieur Pamplemousse waited in vain. There was no indication that Pommes Frites had the slightest intention of joining him. Perhaps, unlike his master, he had managed to grab a bite to eat somewhere, or perhaps he simply didn't fancy what was on the menu; Pommes Frites had never been deeply into pasta. As it was, he had simply disappeared into the night. One moment he was there, the next moment he wasn't. To all intents and purposes the brief incident might never have taken place.

Nevertheless, the sight gave Monsieur Pamplemousse cause for hope. At least he wasn't entirely on his own. He also knew that whatever else happened, Pommes Frites wouldn't let him down. Doubtless he had his own very good reasons for holding his fire.

As a summing-up, it would have pleased Pommes Frites had he been there to share it, for it would have confirmed the rightness of his decision to become the follower rather than the followed; a role for which he was admirably suited.

Pommes Frites' thought processes might have been slow, but nobody could say they weren't thorough. Having, over a period of time, weighed all the facts at his disposal, adding a tiny morsel here, removing another one there, the scales of his computer-like brain had come down heavily on the debit side, and the brief glimpse he'd had of the scene inside the restaurant confirmed his worst fears.

Not for the first time in their long relationship, he found himself entertaining fears about his master's sanity. Hobnobbing with villains was one thing, but actually sitting down to eat with them was something else again.

After such a long and concentrated spell of hard thinking, it was good to be seeing a bit of action again. Time had passed all too slowly since Monsieur Pamplemousse had let him out of the apartment that morning. The first half an hour or so he had spent doing the rounds. Doors opened for him, as they always did; the lady in the *boulangerie* had given him a *croissant* – yesterday's baking if he was any judge, although he was hardly in a position to complain; the man in the *boucherie* had found him a few scraps of beef and veal; but after that there was nothing much else to do except wait patiently in the gardens opposite for his master to make the next move.

That it had all started during the train journey to Paris was beyond doubt. That it had to do with the girl Monsieur Pamplemousse had met was equally obvious. It was an all too familiar pattern of events; the kind of mathematical equation he knew off by heart. Monsieur Pamplemousse + girl = trouble.

From the moment they had stepped off the train things had gone from bad to worse. All in all, Pommes Frites wasn't surprised Madame Pamplemousse appeared to have left home. The only good thing about it was that she hadn't been around to see the state his master had been in when he arrived back that morning – *having been out all night!* Nor had she seen her dress. If she had seen her dress with its tear all the way down the back there would have been hell to pay. Pommes Frites could picture the scene, although he tried very hard not to.

Then there were the baddies. Pommes Frites could tell a baddie from a kilometre away.

Part of his early training with the *Sûreté* had been to sniff them out. It had been one of the easier parts of his induction course and he had passed it with flying colours. Baddies always had a particular odour about them; you could smell them coming before they even turned a corner. The fact that Monsieur Pamplemousse was at that moment sandwiched between two examples of the very worst kind only served to intensify Pommes Frites' resolve. One way and another, for reasons best known to himself, his master had decided to 'go it alone', but that, to Pommes Frites' way of thinking, didn't necessarily mean he shouldn't be around to keep an eye on things, ready to act the moment he was needed.

That moment appeared to have arrived.

The same Saturday evening traffic that had helped him follow his master's 2CV all the way down from Montmartre now worked against him, slowing him down when all he wanted was to reach his destination with all possible speed. Tourists, wandering aimlessly along the pavement in twos and threes, attracted by the lights and the sound of music from Les Halles, conspired to impede his progress. Some even went out of their way to try and stop him.

Tiring of his constant battle against the odds, Pommes Frites took a sharp turn off the boulevard Sebastopol into the rue de Turbigo and entered the underground network of high speed one-way roads which ran below the Forum. Ignoring the hooting of passing motorists, he hugged the side of the tunnel and emerged a few minutes later opposite the Pont Neuf, where he seized the chance to draw breath while waiting for the traffic lights to change in his favour. On familiar territory at long last, it was possible to relax for a moment or two.

Once he had crossed the Seine and reached the safety of the Isle de la Cité, Pommes Frites trotted to the far side, opposite the Left Bank, and then headed off at a brisk pace along the Quai des Orfèvres, confident in his own mind that when he reached his destination his reception would, as always, be welcoming.

His confidence was not misplaced. Seeing him approach, one of the Gendarmes on duty emerged from his perspex sentry box and saluted. Then he gave an inquiring look. Clearly, if Pommes Frites saw fit to arrive on a Saturday night minus his master, something must be very much amiss.

If the reception being accorded to Pommes Frites at the Headquarters of the Paris *Sûreté* came under the heading of 'welcomes, hearty', the same could not be said of the manner in which Monsieur Pamplemousse greeted the arrival at long last of his first course. To say he radiated disappointment would have been to put it mildly.

From the reverential manner in which the owner of the restaurant had borne the food to his table, it looked as though he had been entrusted with some rare and exquisite ambrosial offering contained in a dish made of the most precious and fragile Limoges porcelain imaginable. Monsieur Pamplemousse's taste buds, already on triple time, braced themselves for something special indeed, the spilling of which would have incurred not just the wrath of Mamma Mia, who was anxiously watching her spouse's every movement through the hatch, but the anger of the Gods themselves.

He glared at the china bowl which had been set before him. 'I did not order this,' he exclaimed. 'There must be some mistake.'

'It is a *very* special dish, *signore*. For you. It is *pastino in brodo* – a speciality of the house.'

'There is nothing remotely special about alphabet soup,' growled Monsieur Pamplemousse, 'in this house or in any other. For children, perhaps. But for a fully grown, extremely hungry adult – an adult moreover, who has been promised *spaghetti all'acciuga in salsa d'arancia*, then it is very ordinary!' He looked around the restaurant. 'And if, as you say, it is a speciality of the house, why has no one else ordered it?'

Grasping a spoon, he emphasised each and every point with a jab at the contents of the bowl, causing the liquid to swirl up and engulf the pasta letters until they formed a tangled heap in the centre.

'*Mamma mia!*' The owner clasped his head in both hands, raising his eyes to Heaven.

'Please offer her my apologies,' said Monsieur Pamplemousse, mindful of the fact that it might be wise not to upset the kitchen staff too much, for fear they might try and get their own back later in the meal (Guilot swore he had once witnessed an irate chef in Marseille doing unspeakable things to some *bouillabaisse* destined for a customer who had complained about the quality of his first course), 'but tell her I shall wait for the dish you first recommended.'

'Nota Mamma Mia, my wife,' said the owner unhappily. 'Justa *Mamma mia*!' For some reason he seemed to be losing command of his French. There were beads of perspiration on his forehead.

He glanced apprehensively over his shoulder towards the hatch. From somewhere beyond it there came an impatient clattering of pans. It struck Monsieur Pamplemousse that they were being handled with a considerable amount of undue force. Others in the room sensed it too and looked round to see what was going on.

'Isa good. You try.' Taking Monsieur Pamplemousse's fork, the owner began disentangling the letters, arranging them into a more becoming pattern. Seizing the opportunity, the waitress brought another opened bottle of wine and filled the glass.

Monsieur Pamplemousse relaxed. The Italians did many strange things with pasta, but this had to be the limit. Having said that, hunger began to get the better of him. He picked up the spoon again.

'It is made with the best *pastino*, *signore*.'

'From a box?' said Monsieur Pamplemousse dryly. He realised now what the boy must have been carrying. At least he hadn't been given a child's portion.

He tried a spoonful. It was rather better than he had expected. If the basic component – the *pastino* – was factory made, the other ingredients tasted as though they were fresh from the market; vegetables and red beans, tomatoes, celery . . . some *pesto*. He began to warm to the idea.

As a small boy he had once been taken as a treat to Madame Barattero's Hôtel du Midi in Lamastre. It had been a family occasion, a celebration of some kind – the reason escaped him – but what he remembered most about it was not the *pain d'écrevisses* for which the restaurant was famous, but the fact that Madame Barattero in person had presented him with a dish all to himself. For his special benefit, letters had been added to the broth from a *pot au feu*. It was the first time he had ever come across such a thing, and the first time he realised that food – even in such a revered establishment as the Hôtel du Midi – could be fun. It had sown the seeds for what he was destined to become in later life. Much to everyone's delight he had picked out the words MERCI BEAUCOUP and as a reward had been allowed some red wine out of a glass which was almost too big for him to hold in both hands; the largest he had ever seen at that time.

Lost in a wave of nostalgia, Monsieur Pamplemousse began playing around with the letters, laying them out one by one along the rim of the bowl.

In no time at all he had formed the word GRANDE.

It gave him a certain amount of added pleasure that his actions were clearly causing irritation on either side of him. The two men were watching his efforts with ill-disguised contempt.

'Does he have nothing better to do?'

'Perhaps he thinks we will grow tired of waiting?'

Monsieur Pamplemousse ignored both the comments and the wave of garlic that accompanied them. He was enjoying himself. Clearly, immediate company excepted, he was giving pleasure to others as well. Every so often the owner beamed at him through the hatch, giving the thumbs-up sign whenever their eyes met. Once he was even joined by his wife, who echoed his satisfaction with a nod and a beatific smile. Monsieur Pamplemousse warmed to the couple. You could say what you liked about the Italians, they really appreciated the simple things in life.

After some ten minutes or so he ended up with LU GRANDE MALAISE. It wasn't, perhaps, quite as good as MERCI BEAUCOUP, and his old school teacher would have had something to say about the definite article, but at least it used up another letter and as a definition it summed up his present feelings to a tee: unease, discomfort, unrest.

Spooning up the remaining letters, Monsieur Pample-mousse disposed of them before tucking into the broth. The deed was automatic; it was the Capricorn in him. Neatness came naturally.

The *pastino* felt hard and unyielding, as though it had been baked in an oven. He was glad to have got it out of the way.

Looking up, he realised the owner had joined him. Disappointment, perhaps even a hint of alarm was writ large over the man's face as he gazed down at the half empty bowl.

'There is something wrong?' inquired Monsieur Pample-mousse.

'*Non, non, signore.* Nothing that can not be put right. It

159

is like a game. The permutations are endless. Messages can be made.' Reaching over, the owner began rearranging the letters of the word GRANDE to form DANGER. Then he attacked the others, ending up with ALLE U MA IS.

Monsieur Pamplemousse stared at the result of the manoeuvrings. In the circumstances DANGER seemed a somewhat redundant word: a case of stating the glaringly obvious. As for the rest . . .

'What kind of message is ALLE U MA IS?' he demanded. 'I do not wish to sound complacent, but I feel my arrangement was infinitely preferable. I agree the genders left a lot to be desired, but that is a minor point. At least it made sense . . .'

He broke off as the owner began poking a finger in what was left of his soup.

'You have lost something?' he inquired apprehensively. 'A cuff-link perhaps? A collar stud?'

The man looked puzzled. 'There should be some more *pastino*, *signore*.'

'An "R", a "Z", I think,' said Monsieur Pamplemousse. 'A couple of "A"s – plus a couple of figures – I have forgotten what they all were. It so happens that I have eaten them, but I fail to see . . .'

'You have eaten them? *Christabella, Santa Maria!*' The owner gazed at him in horror. '*Signore!* You not supposed to eat the *pastino*.'

'*Faut pas manger le pastino?*' repeated Monsieur Pamplemousse in a loud voice. 'What kind of a restaurant is it where the *patron* tells you not to eat the food? I see now why there is no mention of your establishment in *Le Guide*. Why should I not eat it?'

'Because, *signore* . . .' Conscious that in the wake of Monsieur Pamplemousse's outburst the other diners – particularly the ones in closest proximity – were hanging on his every word, the owner desperately groped for the right phrase, 'because eating is like music, it is like listening to a symphony. Every note has its place – every quaver – every semi-quaver – remove but one tiny element and you spoil the whole; the message is lost. In this case the message was in the *pastino*.'

Something about the way the man was staring at him, enunciating each and every word with the utmost clarity, caused Monsieur Pamplemousse to stifle the retort he had on the tip of his tongue. *Alors on a compris!* The penny suddenly dropped.

'The message was in the *pastino*?' he repeated.

'*Sì, signore*. In the *pastino*.' The relief on the patron's face was like a burst of sunshine after a storm. He mopped his brow. 'It needs to be savoured, and thought about, and acted upon.'

'In that case,' said Monsieur Pamplemousse, 'perhaps you should bring me another bowl?'

'*Sì, signore. Pronto. Immédiatement.* At once.' He bustled off in the direction of the kitchen only to return almost immediately with a face as long as a stick of *grissini*.

Monsieur Pamplemousse said it for him.

'You have no more soup?'

The man nodded his head miserably. 'It is all gone – and the shop will be closed.'

'That makes it very difficult for you.'

'*Impossible, signore.*'

In desperation, Monsieur Pamplemousse half rose and

glanced towards a sign saying TOILET over a door beyond the kitchen.

Following his thoughts, the two men on either side of him did likewise.

Once again Monsieur Pamplemousse regretted the absence of Pommes Frites. At least Pommes Frites would have stood guard outside the door, stopping the others from following him inside. There might be a window he could climb through, or a chance to pick up some kind of message *en route*. Anything would be an improvement on his present situation. As it was, the two men were watching him like a hawk.

He sat down again. They had him by the short and curlies and no mistake.

'How about the *ossobuco*?' he asked the owner.

'*Si, signore*. I will bring it.' The man shrugged. It was a gesture of defeat.

Monsieur Pamplemousse was made of sterner, more imaginative stuff. Wild ideas of messages inscribed on the bottom of the plate entered his mind. He wondered if the paint would come off with the heat, and if so would it spoil the *ossobuco*. The ink from a felt-tipped pen most certainly would.

Inspiration struck. Thoughts of *ossobuco* reminded him of Pommes Frites and that in turn combined to trigger off a third possibility.

'No!' he exclaimed. 'I have changed my mind. I have had enough. I would not eat here again if I found myself starving to death in the middle of the Sahara desert. The food here is fit only for my dog.'

The owner looked at him as though he had taken leave of his senses. 'But, *signore* . . .'

'I will pay for the rest of the meal,' said Monsieur Pamplemousse slowly and distinctly, 'but I would like to take it home in *un petit sac pour mon chien*: a doggy-bag.'

'Ah! *Sì!*' After a moment's hesitation the owner's face lit up again. '*Sì, sì, signore!* I understand.' Removing the remains of the first course, he disappeared in the direction of the kitchen.

Avoiding the gaze of the men on either side of him, Monsieur Pamplemousse poured himself another glass of wine.

He hadn't long to wait. The prospect of his imminent departure acted as a spur to the speed and quality of the service. He hardly had time to dispose of his wine before the owner reappeared clutching a plastic carrier bag. It felt warm to the touch.

Leave-taking formalities were reduced to a minimum. Offers to pay the bill were waved to one side. The waitress appeared with his coat, holding it open for him as he squeezed his way out from behind the table.

With cries of '*ciao*', '*buona notte*' and '*buona fortuna*' ringing in his ears, Monsieur Pamplemousse left Mamma Mia's, closely followed by the two men. Ignoring their presence, he made his way up the street to where his car was parked. The men's car – a black Chevrolet – was parked almost opposite the restaurant. The fat one climbed into the driving seat, started the engine and reached over to open the passenger door so that Il Blobbo could join him.

Monsieur Pamplemousse went through a pantomime of searching for his keys, then switching on his side-lights and traffic indicators. He made equally heavy weather of extricating his car from its parking space, playing for time as he tried to decide what to do next. Size was on his side; when it came to manoeuvrability his 2CV would win against the other's Chevrolet any day, but once they reached the main boulevards he wouldn't stand an earthly. He turned the rear-view mirror at an angle so that it afforded a clear view of what was going on behind him.

Suddenly, he saw what he had been praying for – lights from an approaching car nosing its way slowly along the narrow street, the driver clearly looking for somewhere to park. Seeing a car was about to leave, he accelerated past the Chevrolet, then pulled up a few metres behind Monsieur Pamplemousse, effectively blocking the way for anyone who might be following.

Monsieur Pamplemousse seized his chance. Switching on the main beams, he put his right foot flat down on the floorboards and wrenched the steering wheel to the left. Clearing one of the iron bollards on the opposite side of the street by a matter of millimetres, he wrenched the wheel to the right again. With a shriek of protesting metal the car bounced off the edge of the kerb and, weaving from side to side, hurtled on its way. Braking sharply at the end, the *deux chevaux* rocked as he made a sharp right turn, then it miraculously righted itself.

In his wake he could hear the sound of blaring horns. It was a very satisfactory noise. The driver of the car wanting to make use of his space looked the kind of person who would take great delight in being as bloody-minded as possible if he were pushed too far.

Following a similar, but parallel, route to the one Pommes Frites had taken earlier in the evening, Monsieur Pamplemousse slowed down to a more leisurely pace. Seeing some traffic lights at red in front of him, he took the first turning right and doubled back into the rabbit warren of streets which made up that corner of Paris.

He was only just in time. As he pulled up behind a lorry making a late-night delivery, he glanced over his shoulder and saw a black Chevrolet shoot past the end of the street. For once he almost wished he drove something slightly less conspicuous than his 2CV. If it had been his pursuers and they were looking the right way they must have seen him. He would be thoroughly boxed in, with no chance of escape.

On the principle of taking no chances, Monsieur Pamplemousse slammed his car into reverse and shot back the way he had come.

Regardless of oncoming traffic swerving to avoid both him and each other, ignoring other drivers hooting and gesticulating at his seemingly imbecilic behaviour, he crossed the busy boulevard Sebastopol at speed.

Reverting to his head level with the dashboard mode of driving, he carried on until he found a suitable turning, then he made good his escape. Only then, as he slowed down to open the side window and let in a welcome draught of cold air, did he realise he was sweating like a pig.

On the corner of rue de Turbigo a gendarme reached for his portable radio.

'It is the phantom *deux chevaux* again!'

'*C'est la vie!*' That was the way it went. Sometimes you spent hours doing nothing. Then everything happened at once. First a driverless car going backwards up a main artery. Then, even as he spoke, he saw another one approaching. It was doing exactly the same thing – only this time he could see both driver and passenger.

The second car had a Rome registration, so what else could you expect? Fortunately he was able to give the girl at the other end both sets of numbers.

9

CATCH 22bis

Monsieur Pamplemousse replaced the telephone handset
and stood for a moment or two staring out of the kiosk,
lost in thought.

The conversation had been short and to the point. As
short and to the point in its way, as had been the message
contained in the doggy bag. Wrapped in silver foil to
protect it from the *ossobuco* and with the missing letters
inserted, it had spelled out the words: DANGER: ALLEZ
AU MARAIS. Underneath it there was an address in the
Place des Vosges.

It was yet another case of reason flying out the window.
The Marais was the last area of Paris where he would have
chosen to look: the Place des Vosges at that! Unarguably,
with its central fountain and its carefully tended sym-
metrical gardens, it was one of the most beautiful squares
in Paris. The perfectly proportioned town houses surrounding it on all four sides, with their arched stone
arcades at ground level and their dormer windows and
steeply pitched slate roofs above, gave it an air of discreet

respectability. It was hard to picture 'goings on' behind the elegant red-brick façades of the upper storeys. Or was it? Perhaps that same air of respectability would add a certain *cachet*. It would undoubtedly up the prices!

Below the message telling him where to go there was a hastily scrawled telephone number: first the 19 code for International, then 39 for Italy, followed by a Sicilian number, with instructions to dial it at 20.00 precisely.

A woman had answered, almost before the first ring was completed. She must have had her hand poised on the receiver. She had spoken quickly and clearly, and from her manner and tone of voice Monsieur Pamplemousse formed the opinion that she was in fear of being overheard. It had sounded like a cry from the heart, an act of desperation on the part of someone who had swallowed her pride and knew there was no going back.

Conscious of all that, and aware that after his long conversation with the Director when he had telephoned from the Gare de Lyon there weren't many units left on his *télécarte*, he had listened and taken careful note, interjecting only when it was absolutely necessary.

'Were you responsible for "springing" me after I was arrested?' he inquired.

'You are the only one I can turn to or trust. Caterina has spoken of you to my cousin at the restaurant, who phoned me.'

It was said as though it had been the simplest problem in the world, but he couldn't help wondering how she had got to hear of his plight so quickly. It was no time to go into details.

'Mamma Mia is your cousin?'

'Maria is my cousin. I would not wish either her or her husband to be involved any more than they have been already.'

'How can you be sure that what you have told me is true?'

'Because Caterina is my daughter, and I know her – perhaps better than she knows herself. Besides, I am a woman and I am from Sicily. Women in Sicily are told nothing, yet we know everything.

'It has always been so. Our men have protected us. Their wife, their family, it is the most important thing in their life. They say they know what is best.'

'I, too, have someone who is dear to me and who is often told nothing, but who knows all,' said Monsieur Pamplemousse, in an effort to establish a common bond.

'It is not the same,' said the woman. 'Believe me, it is not the same. Your wife has her freedom. In Sicily that is not so.

'In Sicily, the men can do as they please provided they are not found out. But things are changing slowly. Women here are starting to rebel. They want to go out into the world too.

'I have always had everything I could possibly wish for in the way of money ... clothes ... everything except freedom. That is the most precious thing of all, and that is what I want for Caterina.'

'But it has to be used wisely?'

'Exactly. It is not good to run before you can walk. That is why I need your help. You must do whatever it costs.'

'There is no price, *signora*. I will simply do my best. That is all I can do.'

'*Grazie*. I will tell you...' She was in the middle of speaking again when there was a click and the line went dead. It was the moment of truth and no mistake.

Monsieur Pamplemousse climbed back into his 2CV and switched on the engine. Heading south and using back streets as far as possible, he drove slowly through the relatively deserted 3rd *arrondissement* while he considered his next move.

Despite the modest pace at which he was travelling, or perhaps because of it, his progress didn't go unreported. Space in the airwaves above Paris soon became at a premium.

Finally abandoning his car in a side street near the rue des Francs-Bourgeois Rivoli – the main thoroughfare leading into the Place des Vosges, Monsieur Pamplemousse set off on foot. He felt less conspicuous that way. He hadn't gone very far before he realised the wisdom of his move. As he drew near the *Place* he was nearly run down by a car reversing at speed. He only just managed to jump clear in time.

'*Poule!* Where do you think you are going?'

'*Voilà! Les flics.*' The driver had his window wound down. He looked anxiously over his shoulder as he drove on his way, more concerned for his own well-being than for any passing pedestrians who were foolish enough to walk in the road. It was asking for trouble.

Where he had just been, a group of *gendarmes* were flagging down the traffic, peering into car windows, scrutinising the occupants.

Monsieur Pamplemousse stood for a moment in a shop doorway while he considered the matter. Perhaps they were expecting more trouble after the International, or maybe there was some kind of 'happening' in the Place de la Bastille. The former was hardly likely – it was too much off the beaten track – the latter was too far away.

Playing it by ear, he backtracked and made a short détour towards the rue de Rivoli, entering the Place des Vosges through a side street. On the way he passed three long grey buses filled with CRS riot police. There were two *gendarmes* standing inside the archway at the entrance to the square, but they paid him scant attention. They were far more interested in the solitary occupant of a large Mercedes trying to leave. The car had a CD plate and the man was protesting in no uncertain terms.

The restaurant Coconnas to his right was full. Light streamed from its windows and he could see waiters hurrying about their business, but beyond it, towards the house where Victor Hugo had once lived and worked, there was a patch of relative darkness. Some way beyond that again, Monsieur Pamplemousse found the number he was looking for. There was a modern coded entry-lock, but it must have been disconnected, for when he pushed against the huge wooden door it swung open easily and he found himself entering a small, paved courtyard.

Approaching an ornate front door, he pressed an unlabelled bell push let into the wall beneath one of a pair of wrought-iron lamps.

The door was opened almost immediately by a young girl. She was wearing school clothes – a gym slip and blouse. If the intention had been to conceal what little else she might be wearing underneath, both garments

171

were several sizes too small. Her cheeks were heavily rouged and she carried a hockey stick. There was music playing in the background and he could hear the clink of glasses and the sound of laughter coming from a room nearby.

'I wish to speak to the "*Madame*".'

'Do you have an invitation?'

'*Non.*'

The girl hesitated. 'I'm dreadfully sorry . . .' She spoke with a cultivated English accent.

'It is I who am sorry,' said Monsieur Pamplemousse firmly. 'The "*Madame*", *s'il vous plaît.*'

After a moment's hesitation the girl led him towards a flight of wide, richly carpeted stairs. Monsieur Pamplemousse reflected that it was interesting the difference clothes and subdued lighting made to a person. Dressed the way she was, she didn't look more than fourteen or fifteen years old. As they mounted the first few stairs, he averted his gaze, glancing instead through an open door to his right. He registered all he needed to know.

What was it President Mitterrand had once said? 'If Ministers resigned because of their peccadillos I would lose half my cabinet overnight.' It looked as though the other half might be in imminent danger too. He recognised several well-known faces from other walks of life.

The girl tried several doors on the first landing. The first two were locked. Someone was attempting to play the hornpipe on an accordion behind one, the sound of rattling chains came from the second room.

'My name's Deirdre, by the way,' said the girl. She tried another door. 'Third time lucky!'

'*Sacré bleu!*' Following her into the room, Monsieur Pamplemousse narrowly escaped being struck on the head by a naked man swinging upside down on a trapeze. A girl kneeling on a bed in the centre of the room looked round. 'Shut the door, Deirdre. There's a draught.'

'*C'est impossible!*' Monsieur Pamplemousse stared at the scene.

'Nothing is impossible with Ernestine,' said Deirdre. 'She's Hungarian. Her parents owned a travelling circus. They were always on the move. Would you like to have a go? It's super fun.'

'*Non, merci,*' said Monsieur Pamplemousse hastily. 'I am afraid I do not have a head for heights.'

'How about the banisters?' Deirdre, who seemed to have a penchant for *non sequiturs*, licked her lips and ran her hands down the highly polished surface. 'You can get up quite a speed if you start from the top.'

Monsieur Pamplemousse winced. He was still feeling the effects of his outing the night before.

'I am not sure I would know what to do when I got to the bottom,' he said.

Deirdre giggled. 'It's easy when you know how.' She hitched up her skirt. 'Don't worry. I'll show you.'

'Is there no pleasure in simplicity any more?' asked Monsieur Pamplemousse. 'Besides, when I said I am in a hurry, I meant just that.'

He stood back to allow another girl free passage. It struck him that she didn't take as much advantage of his move as she might have done. She was sucking something nameless on the end of a stick and as she squeezed past him he smelt aniseed; aniseed and what could have been Chanel 19. It was a strangely disturbing combination.

The room the first girl took him to was at the front of the building. It was lavishly furnished in the style of the period. Whoever lived in the house must be wealthy beyond most people's wildest dreams. Thick wooden beams supporting the high ceilings were ornately inlaid with other woods. From the central beam there hung a sizeable unlit chandelier.

Deirdre glanced up. 'Would you like a "freebie" while you're waiting?'

'I am in a hurry,' said Monsieur Pamplemousse.

'A "quickie" then?'

'There comes a time in a man's life,' said Monsieur Pamplemousse with a sigh, 'when the word "quickie" betrays a certain degree of optimism.'

'I don't mind waiting.'

'Please. There is no time to lose.'

For one awful moment he thought she was going to cry, then the door closed behind her.

Left on his own at long last, Monsieur Pamplemousse crossed to the window and parted the curtains slightly. If anything, police activity was on the increase. More *gendarmes* were now stationed just inside the arcade on the west side, where they were able to keep an eye on traffic entering the square. The only other way in, except on foot, was through an archway directly opposite the one he had just used. From a policing point of view the layout of the square couldn't have been better. There were just two ways in – from the north and from the west, and two ways out – to the east and to the south.

'What are you doing here?'

He turned at the sound of a voice. 'I think I might ask you the same question.'

'I presume you know the truth – otherwise you wouldn't be here.'

Monsieur Pamplemousse gazed long and hard at Caterina. In the glow of the soft pink light from table lamps scattered about the room she looked positively ravishing. Even more so, he had to admit, than when he had last seen her on the train. She was wearing an ivory coloured dress of a simplicity which only came when expense was no object. With her hair up, she had an air of authority beyond her years. It made him feel momentarily sad.

He motioned her to sit. It was no time for beating about the bush.

'I have just had a long conversation with your *mamma*. She applauds what you have done, but now she wants you to come home. If you stay it will lead to nothing but unhappiness, to tragedy even; to a war within the "family" itself.'

'I am sorry. It is too late.'

'You realise your *papà* will be forced to kill you.'

'Me?' Caterina laughed, but it was clear a chill had entered into her. 'That is not possible. He would never do such a thing.' For the first time she avoided his gaze.

'He would have no choice,' said Monsieur Pamplemousse. 'He is bound by the code of the Cosa Nostra. He has been "baptised"; he has sworn an oath, he has undergone the ritual, mixing the blood of his trigger finger with the blood of others. You of all people should know, from that moment on the Mafia Family took precedence over his own, even if it means killing his only daughter. That is the rule. It is a total requirement and there is no escaping the fact. He would demand it of others, and he would expect them to obey the rule without question. Therefore, as a Man of Honour, he cannot possibly escape it himself.

'You have committed one of the worst sins of all – a whole series, in fact. You have disobeyed his orders, and what you are doing is something that in itself will bring disgrace.'

Monsieur Pamplemousse's thoughts went back to the conversation he'd had with Caterina's mother and a question he had posed: 'Why are you telling me all this?'

'Because I want Caterina back and I want the explanations – the pressure – to come from someone else. If this thing leaks out it will kill her father.'

He sat down beside Caterina and placed a hand on hers. 'You must close down. Now. This moment.'

'But I can't. It is the opening night.'

'Then it must also, I fear, be the closing night. Apart from anything else, from what I have seen in the very short time I have been here, you have managed to accumulate enough "names" to promote the biggest scandal that has hit France for many years.'

'What if I refuse? You cannot make me.'

'You are right. I cannot make you. But if you go ahead, then just as surely as night follows day, you will be responsible for the death of your father. Even if he goes against his own code – the code of the Cosa Nostra – and if others let that be, which is unlikely, he will be unable to stand the disgrace. A daughter who disobeys his commands? A daughter who runs away without permission to do her own thing? A daughter who opens a bordello in Paris?

'You know what they would say? They would say he

176

was no better than a pimp. A pimp, living on his daughter's earnings. For someone with his background there could be no greater insult.'

It was, thought Monsieur Pamplemousse, yet another case of Catch 22 with a vengeance. Catch 22bis.

'But can it not wait? Until the end of this evening at least. I cannot go back on my promises . . .'

'Promises to whom? The worst that can happen is that you will leave behind a lot of unsatisfied customers; unsatisfied in the truest sense of the word. They will probably take it out on their subordinates in the morning, but so what?'

Caterina shrugged, then she looked around. 'It has been a lot of work for nothing. What do you think of it all?'

'Banisters will never be the same again,' said Monsieur Pamplemousse. 'It has also given me a whole new perspective on lollipops.'

'No, seriously.'

'Seriously . . .' Monsieur Pamplemousse crossed to the window again and parted the thick curtains. 'Look!'

He raised his hands as Caterina joined him. 'It is not of my doing, believe me.'

'Then who?'

'I do not know. It is of no consequence. We are dealing in facts. And the fact is, unless we leave now you will be in serious trouble, and so shall I. They will throw the book at me.'

Monsieur Pamplemousse looked at her curiously. 'You ask me what I think. I think you have done much in a very short time. In some respects I am lost in admiration.'

'It was very easy really. The house is empty. It belongs

177

to a member of my family – an uncle. Mamma spoke of him many times. He is out of the country.'

'And the girls? How many are there?'

'Fifteen.'

'*Fifteen!* Where do they all come from?'

'That was the least of the problems. You forget – I attend a convent school.'

Monsieur Pamplemousse suppressed a whistle. No wonder the place threatened to be such an instant success. It must be quite unique in the annals of *maisons de débauches*.

'Do you realise the risk you are running? There are other ways of proving yourself. You have your whole life before you. It is pointless to gain your freedom only to lose it again. Besides, remember what happened to the Dugong . . . there is such a thing as being too successful.'

While he was talking, he ushered Caterina out of the room. 'Round up the rest of the girls – as quickly and as quietly as possible. Tell them to get dressed. I will see you outside.'

Giving her no time to argue, Monsieur Pamplemousse hastened down the stairs and let himself out into the arcade.

He looked to his right and then to his left, trying to decide what to do for the best. Shadowy figures made their way round the perimeter of the *Place*, but now he was on ground level again it all looked relatively quiet. Only the stationary headlamps from waiting cars and vans on the north side gave a clue to the activity that was going on. By their light he could see passers-by being asked for their *cartes d'identité*.

Fifteen girls! Sixteen, if you included Caterina – and he

had no intention of leaving without her. Even in small groups they would never make it without being stopped. It was like a war-time operation. No one was being spared.

Monsieur Pamplemousse's attention was momentarily diverted by a burst of flash guns further along on his side of the *Place*. A party of Japanese tourists, streaming out of a *café*, were boarding a parked coach through a door in its side, taking photographs of each other as they went. Photographs of each other and ... Monsieur Pamplemousse gave a start.

To his astonishment he saw Pommes Frites posing alongside one member of the group. Not so much directing operations, but clearly taking an active interest in what was going on. He had an extraordinary capacity for putting in an appearance when it was least expected. It was quite uncanny.

Whether it was the flashlights, or simply a case of built-in extrasensory perception was hard to say, but Pommes Frites caught sight of Monsieur Pamplemousse at almost exactly the same moment, and came bounding towards him full of the joy of his discovery.

He looked pleased with himself, as well he might, since in his way he was partly responsible for bringing together and coordinating the forces not only of those who were looking for his master, but those who, coincidentally, were even now about to home in on the clandestine activities in the Place des Vosges. For all its outward aloofness, the Marais was like a village. News travelled fast.

That the two events were not necessarily compatible didn't cross Pommes Frites' mind as he exchanged greetings with his master. As far as he was concerned, their meeting up was sufficient in itself.

'Wait.' Seeing the door open behind him, Monsieur Pamplemousse signalled both Pommes Frites and Caterina to stay where they were.

Brushing past the last of the Japanese tourists, he approached the front of the coach and tapped on the door. Receiving no response, he slid it open. The driver was laid back, feet on the dashboard, a cigarette dangling from his mouth.

Waving his *Guide* pass with an authority learned in the *Sûreté* and developed over years of dealing with some of Paris's worst criminal elements, who thought they knew all the answers, Monsieur Pamplemousse glared at the man. His first thought had been that they might all beg a lift, but something told him he wouldn't get very far with that idea. He decided to try another tack.

'Do you see anything strange about the way you are parked, *Monsieur*?'

The driver didn't even bother to remove the cigarette. '*Non*. Why should I? This is where I always park.'

'Half on the pavement? In an area where coaches are expressly forbidden to park?'

'*Oui*.' The man made play of looking out of his window. 'What would you have me do – stay in the rue des Francs-Bourgeois and cause an *impasse*?'

Monsieur Pamplemousse jerked a thumb over his shoulder. 'Out,' he barked, dropping any pretence at politeness. 'I am booking you for illegal parking. Furthermore, I am also booking you for causing an obstruction and for being in charge of an unsafe vehicle.'

'Unsafe?' Brushing ash from his jacket, the driver

clambered out of the coach and joined Monsieur Pamplemousse on the pavement. 'It is brand new. It was
delivered from the factory only two weeks ago. It has two
toilets, a bar, video, air-conditioning, walk-in luggage
space, tinted windows.'

Monsieur Pamplemousse withdrew his notebook from
the concealed fold in his trousers and flipped it open. 'A
flat tyre on the nearside rear wheel.'

The man kicked it. 'I have no flat tyre.'

Monsieur Pamplemousse removed his Cross ballpoint
pen from an inside pocket, gave the barrel a quick twist,
and then applied the pointed end to a valve. There was a
satisfying hiss of escaping air. Fortunately for his purpose
the wheel was one of a pair. The coach would still be
driveable.

'*Merde!*' Leaving the man gazing disbelievingly at his
tyre, Monsieur Pamplemousse strolled in leisurely fashion
round to the back of the vehicle. He was beginning to
enjoy himself. It was quite like old times. 'One defective
rear light.'

'*Morbleu!*' bellowed the man as he joined him. 'That is
nonsense! Look at them!'

Monsieur Pamplemousse lifted his foot. There was a
crash of splintering plastic and the light went out. He
turned to a new page.

'Telling lies. Arguing with those in authority. I
wouldn't be in your shoes. Wait till I get you back to the
station. The Squad for the Protection of Tourists may
have other ideas.'

Having carefully made sure none of the police were
looking his way, Monsieur Pamplemousse mimed waving
to an imaginary colleague, going through a routine of

whistle blowing and holding a telephone to his ear. As an *encore* he made a throat-cutting gesture followed by the classic sign for 'at the double'.

Out of the corner of his eye he saw Pommes Frites watching his every movement. The worried expression had returned. Clearly, he was of the opinion that his master was suffering from another relapse; possibly permanent this time.

'Look here...' Unbelievably the *salaud* was still attempting to bluster his way out.

Monsieur Pamplemousse pointed towards the rue de Rivoli. 'Waiting there are three van loads of CRS. One more peep out of you, my friend, and I shall hand you over. They have been doing nothing all day and they will enjoy a little diversion; a chance to flex their muscles. It will be like feeding time at the zoo. They are not gentlemen like me.'

It did the trick, as he knew it would.

With considerable ill grace, the driver reached for his wallet.

Monsieur Pamplemousse grabbed hold of the man's jacket lapels and slammed him against the side of the coach. His action triggered off another series of photographs, this time from inside the vehicle. White faces pressed against the inside of the glass as they waited for their flash-guns to recharge.

'*Imbecile!*' He took the note from the man and slipped it into his trouser pocket. 'Never do that in the open. People will think the worst.'

He pointed to the *café*. 'Wait in there. I will see what I can do, but I warn you – 100 francs will not go very far.'

As the man disappeared, Monsieur Pamplemousse

turned and waved to Caterina. 'Quick! Get everyone into the coach.'

Ignoring the flood of girls pouring out of the house, he went round to the front and climbed into the driving seat. Compared with his 2CV it was the ultimate in sophistication; more like the cockpit of a jumbo jet. He made a stab at some switches. The windscreen washer came on, the sound of soft music filled the air, and the interior lights went out. A murmur of oriental approval rose from behind.

'Where are you taking us?' Caterina boarded the coach and slid the door shut behind her.

'Where do you think?' asked Monsieur Pamplemousse. 'To the Gare de Lyon.'

He peered at the controls and made another stab at starting the engine. This time he struck lucky. It roared into life.

As they moved off, Pommes Frites stationed himself behind the windscreen alongside his master and Caterina picked up a microphone. She switched it on. 'What would you like me to say?'

'Anything,' said Monsieur Pamplemousse. 'How about "The safety instructions are in the back of the seat in front of you" or "Be careful when you open the overhead luggage compartments. Heavy objects might fall out"? No-one is going to know any different.'

Seeing the exit he was heading for was temporarily blocked, he made a snap decision to go round the Place des Vosges a second time. Apart from anything else, it would give him a chance to familiarise himself with the controls. He mopped his brow. The interior of the coach was like an oven.

'Try turning off the heating,' hissed Caterina. 'The Marais,' she continued, for the benefit of those behind, 'is a maze of squares, many of which in time begin to look exactly the same.'

'Tell the girls to lie down,' said Monsieur Pample-mousse, as he completed his circuit and began making a second approach. 'Whatever happens they must not be seen.'

Caterina switched off the microphone. 'I do not think that will be necessary.'

Something about the wistful tone of her voice made Monsieur Pamplemousse look round. He saw what she meant. Feet rather than heads protruded above the top of the seats. His knowledge of Japanese was non-existent, but what little sound he could hear above the music seemed to be registering pleasure rather than complaints.

As they turned the corner leading to the eastern exit of the square, he gave a loud blast on the horn and slid open his window.

'*S'il vous plaît, monsieur. S'il vous plaît.*'

The *gendarme* nearest the coach tapped on one of the windows, registered an inscrutable face staring back at him, and having received a blinding flash straight in the eyes for his pains, uttered an oath and hastily waved them on.

Monsieur Pamplemousse breathed a sigh of relief as he accelerated away. At least he would have more room to manoeuvre once they reached the safety of the Boulevard Beaumarchais. The possibility of their becoming inextricably jammed between a couple of bollards, or worse still, wedged in one of the many arcades had never been far from his mind.

It was as they joined the never-ending stream of traffic circulating round the central column in the Place de la Bastille – the very moment when he needed all his concentration – that Caterina suddenly broke off from her commentary and shrieked a warning into the microphone. It was accompanied by a loud growl from Pommes Frites as he launched himself into space.

Monsieur Pamplemousse braked sharply. Aware of a commotion going on behind him, but surrounded on all sides by fast-moving traffic, he accelerated again, switching off his mind to all but the task in hand as he jockeyed for position in order to enter the rue de Lyon before the lights changed.

At one point he felt a draught of cold air down the back of his neck, and heard renewed squeals of brakes behind them, but by then he was long past caring. Never had the lights above the Gare de Lyon seemed more welcoming.

Ignoring rumbles of discontent from waiting taxi drivers, he parked the coach as close to the main entrance as it was possible to get and climbed out of his seat.

'Wait here.'

The clock in the tower still couldn't make up its mind as whether it was midday or four-twenty. His own watch said twenty-one thirty-seven. He dashed into the station and was outside again by twenty-one thirty-nine. Caterina was waiting for him by the open door of the coach.

'There is a train to Rome leaving at twenty-two hundred hours. You will need to change at Milan. Hurry – there isn't much time.'

'Have you enough money?' Monsieur Pamplemousse looked inside the coach. It was a redundant question.

Large quantities of notes seemed to be changing hands all round.

'You were wonderful,' said Caterina. '*Papà* would have been proud of you.'

'*Merci.*' It struck Monsieur Pamplemousse as a dubious compliment, but he suddenly realised the tour leader was trying to address him.

'Excuse, please . . . *s'il vous plaît.*'

'What is it?' asked Monsieur Pamplemousse impatiently. He seemed fated not to say a proper goodbye to Caterina.

'Hope we did right thing with strangers in coach.'

Monsieur Pamplemousse stared at the man in bewilderment. 'Strangers? What strangers? Where?'

'Two men dressed in black. Not part of tour. All right now. They gone.'

'Gone?' repeated Monsieur Pamplemousse.

'We make them offer they cannot refuse.' For a split second the semblance of a smile crossed the other's face.

'What happened?'

'They refuse offer. Great shame.' The man made a throat-cutting gesture.

'But where are they?' repeated Monsieur Pamplemousse impatiently.

The tour leader made a gesture towards the back of the coach. 'Make use of emergency exit. Much traffic in Paris this time of night. Especially round what you call Place Bastille. They will not bother you again.'

Looking back down the centre aisle, Monsieur Pamplemousse realised to his horror that the *Issue de Secours* window was wide open. It was no wonder he had felt a draught down the back of his neck. Inscrutable faces gazed back at him and cameras were raised yet again. There was a series of flashes. First one, then another. It was followed by a whole barrage.

'We have saying in Japan – "It is good when man's deeds express his thoughts." We take quick vote and our thoughts all as one. By same token, sometimes best to be saying nothing afterwards.'

'The Japanese have much wisdom,' said Monsieur Pamplemousse. 'I have already forgotten our conversation.'

'Family are happy for you.'

'The *Family*? You do not mean . . .'

'No, not what you are thinking. Not the *Yakuza* – not Japanese Mafia. Family of brothers from company sports club. We all black belts. It is our reward for highest output ever – one week in your wonderful city. Already we have seen *Folies Bergère*, Lido, Moulin Rouge and many night spots. This part, with lovely young hostesses best of all. Come as big surprise – not included in itinerary. Round things off and no mistake.'

The tour leader handed Monsieur Pamplemousse a hat. It felt heavy.

'We offer many thanks in gratitude. Have no need of loose change any more.

'Staff of Nagihuku return to lathes happy men. Output go up.

'Best part of holiday. Better holiday than last year – three weeks in Saigon. Men wonder what will happen to them next year.'

At a given signal, cameras flashed again and there was a polite round of applause.

Monsieur Pamplemousse acknowledged it with a bow.

As he did so a feeling of guilt came over him. 'Were you planning to visit any other nightspots?'

'No. We all worn out. Only nightspot we visit now is bed.' Again there was a flicker of a smile. 'Leave for Japan by early flight in morning.'

'I will telephone the *café*,' said Monsieur Pamplemousse, 'and arrange for the driver to return you to your hotel.'

'All good things come to end,' said the tour leader. 'But we return home with good memories.'

'You must take care of them,' said Monsieur Pamplemousse. 'In France, we have a saying: *Les bons souvenirs sont des bijoux perdus* – Good memories are lost jewels.'

He looked towards the station entrance, but Caterina and her friends had long since disappeared.

'Nice girl,' said the man.

'Very,' said Monsieur Pamplemousse.

10

LE TRAIN BLEU

Monsieur Pamplemousse paused at the foot of the marble staircase leading up to Le Restaurant Train Bleu. He hesitated, wondering whether or not to take the plunge. The tables and chairs outside the *brasserie* on the main concourse below the restaurant were crowded with people aware of trains to catch. The *Grande Salle* would be a much more leisurely affair. The other diners would mostly be there for the food, not because they were going anywhere. Pommes Frites decided for him. He bounded on ahead as though the matter were a foregone conclusion.

'*Deux personnes, Monsieur?*' One of several black-suited *maîtres d'hôtel* came forward and took in the situation at a glance.

'Is it possible to have a table in the window? One with a view of the *quai*.'

The man made a sucking noise through his teeth.

Monsieur Pamplemousse did something he had never, ever done before and probably never would again – the Chief would throw a fit if he knew – but he suddenly felt too tired to care. Besides, without making heavy weather of it, he wanted to be absolutely certain Caterina was carrying out his wishes.

'*Le Guide* would consider it a great favour.'

It did the trick. It wouldn't make any difference to the outcome of his report, of course, and anyway he would meet that hurdle when it came.

An elderly waiter arrived with the menu, then a young *commis* brought a bread roll. The first waiter somehow went with the restaurant. But then, looking around, so did most of the staff. Much more so than the *Echiré* butter, wrapped in gold foil.

Monsieur Pamplemousse gazed out of the window. He hadn't long to wait. A crocodile of demure looking schoolgirls appeared from somewhere out of the depths and wound its way towards a waiting train. Whoever was hearing confession on the morrow was in for a busy time.

Was it his imagination or did the girl at the head of the file turn and look up? He would have given anything to have had his Leitz Trinovids with him so that he could bring the whole thing into sharp focus. He resisted the temptation to rush down the stairs and say a last goodbye. Not with others around. Caterina probably wouldn't thank him for it.

The first waiter reappeared with pad and pencil at the ready. He looked as though he was anxious to get home and rest his feet.

'It is sad when they have to go away, *Monsieur*.'

'Very sad,' said Monsieur Pamplemousse.

'*Mademoiselle* is going far?'

'To Rome. Possibly beyond.'

'Beyond Rome!' The man made it sound like a journey to the moon.

Perhaps realising the fact, he gave a sigh. 'It is nothing nowadays. In my day, Lyon and the Mediterranean seemed far away and magical. Then there were trains with romantic names like Mistral; in July the *quais* would be full of wives going south for the long summer holidays – or to their lovers. Husbands would wave goodbye and go back to their offices and their mistresses until August came.'

'It is hard to picture now,' said Monsieur Pamplemousse. 'The young go everywhere. It is the modern way.'

'Everything is the same – like *Eurosucre*,' said the waiter. 'We, too, have been modernised. The new kitchens are . . . *poof!*' He waved towards the service area. 'What shall I say? It is like comparing a luxury coach with a 2CV.'

'That, of course, depends on the driver,' said Monsieur Pamplemousse. 'Some are adept at both.' He picked up the menu and made a pretence of studying it.

The waiter leaned over to help. 'I can recommend the *assiette gourmande "Train Bleu"*, *Monsieur. Foie gras, melon, saumon fumé, rillette de saumon, salade*.

'Afterwards, perhaps I might suggest fresh leg of lamb roasted the *Forézienne* way, with mushrooms and diced potatoes sautéd in butter and truffles. It has always been a speciality of the restaurant.'

Truffles again! Monsieur Pamplemousse gladly surrendered the decision-making to another. Compared with the ones he had eaten the other evening they would be only a token gesture – discarded peelings probably, but nonetheless welcome for that. From now on he would always think of Caterina when he ate them. Perhaps he should have asked her mother to pay him in 'black diamonds'? A whole lorry load! Except he knew he was being facetious.

'And to drink, *Monsieur*?'

Monsieur Pamplemousse turned the menu over and consulted the wine list on the back.

'A Côte Rotie "Les Jumelles".' He had more or less begun with a Côte Rotie; it would be fitting to end with one. Although, once again, he doubted if it would equal his own bottle. At least he would be able to give it his full attention this time round.

'*Parfait!*' The waiter beamed his approval. 'An excellent choice, *Monsieur*. You will not be disappointed.' He spoke with the authority of one who seldom drank anything else.

'*Monsieur* would like some water?'

'An *eau de Vichy*,' said Monsieur Pamplemousse. 'It will be good for my digestion.' He was tempted to ask for one of the Director's dry martinis, but he thought better of it and ordered a Kir instead.

'*Vin blanc, Monsieur*, or *Royale*?'

'*Royale*. No, on second thoughts, leave out the cassis. Make it a straight champagne.' Why not? He was suddenly feeling very flat and the champagne would give him a lift.

As the waiter disappeared, Monsieur Pamplemousse reached for his notebook. It was back to work again.

He looked around at the setting. Built at the time of the Paris Exhibition of 1900 and now classed as a National monument, the whole restaurant was a memorial to the carefree life of *la Belle Époque*; overwhelming in its extravagant decadence. The Baroque gilded pillars supporting the vaulted ceilings were a riot of rococo, scantily clad, Rubenesque female figures – not a straight line among them. The ceiling itself and the surrounding walls, all newly restored, had been covered by artists of the day with murals depicting romantic scenes of the times: men wearing straw hats and women in long, frilly dresses, or views which might be seen from the windows of Train Bleu itself by those who were taking the route to the sun and the Côte d'Azur.

Everything about it was sumptuous. The rich, buttoned leather *banquettes* and dark red hanging drapes, the chairs and the tables with their spotless white linen cloths, the vast chandeliers overhead, the ornate coat stands surmounted by lamps, the heavy polished brass, all served to remind those using the restaurant of a bygone age. Eating in Le Train Bleu was as much an architectural as a gastronomic experience. *Le Guide*'s symbols would be stretched to their limit.

Monsieur Pamplemousse suddenly became aware of a shadow materialising beside him and he felt a kiss on the back of his neck. It sent shivers down his spine.

'I must run,' said Caterina. 'It is only to say thank you.'

'Thank *you*,' said Monsieur Pamplemousse. 'And *bonne chance* – whatever you do – wherever you go.'

'I will write!'

'That would be nice,' said Monsieur Pamplemousse. But he knew she wouldn't, and it might be just as well.

The waiter arrived back carrying a bottle of wine.

'*Monsieur*'s daughter?'

Monsieur Pamplemousse shook his head. 'Not even a Goddaughter . . . I'm afraid.' He almost added 'yet' as an afterthought.

'Aaah!' It was the long drawn out response of one who had seen many things in his time. 'Young men have visions, *Monsieur*. Old men have dreams.' He withdrew the cork, sniffed it briefly, and with an air of approval placed it in a dish alongside the bottle, pocketing the foil. Then he poured a little of the wine, swirled it round the glass, and placed it back on the table.

'*Monsieur?*'

It was, thought Monsieur Pamplemousse, arguably the best Côte Rotie he had ever tasted. Soft, heady, assertive and surprisingly mature for its age, with plenty of body, fruity ... But then, didn't that go to prove his long-held theory: wine, a living thing, tasted of many things besides the grapes that went into its making, not least being the company you kept and all that went with it.

He placed the hat he had been given on the table in front of him.

'You may keep the change,' he said grandly. 'In the meantime, please look after the table. We shall be back in a moment.'

If they hurried he would be just in time to wave the Palatino goodbye.

'You were very restless in your sleep last night, Aristide,' said Madame Pamplemousse. 'Was it something you had for dinner?'

'No, *Couscous*,' said Monsieur Pamplemousse. 'If anything it was something I didn't have.'

'Did you miss me while I was away?'

'Of course I did, Doucette. I always do. You know that. The apartment is very quiet without you.'

'I tried to telephone you several times, but it was either engaged or there was no answer.'

That summed up the last few days to a tee.

Madame Pamplemousse concentrated on dusting a picture near the window. 'You didn't eat half the things I left you.'

Monsieur Pamplemousse resisted the temptation to say,

'But I ate the other half.' He changed the subject instead.

'How is Agathe?' It would be good for ten minutes at least. Agathe would complain if she had nothing to complain about.

He had arrived home late the previous evening to find Doucette already in bed and asleep. Climbing in beside her, his mind swarming with all the things that had happened during the day, he had fully expected to lie awake for hours. Instead of which he had fallen asleep almost as soon as his head touched the pillow, and he was only now beginning to come out of it.

'That man I was telling you about is still there.' Madame Pamplemousse was in the middle of listing her sister's woes when she broke off and stared out of the window.

Prowling round the apartment, looking to see if he had left anything lying about which might be hard to explain – a photograph of Caterina, *par exemple*, or the remains of dinner for two, Monsieur Pamplemousse paused.

'What man?'

'The one I was telling you about at breakfast,' said Madame Pamplemousse impatiently. 'The one on crutches. You don't listen to a word I say sometimes.' She opened the door to the balcony in order to get a better view.

'He's hardly moved since I first saw him, although that's not surprising. Poor man. How he manages to play anything at all with his legs in plaster and his head all bandaged up like it is, I don't know. I suppose he's a musician. He wouldn't be carrying a violin case otherwise.'

She glanced back over her shoulder. 'He keeps looking up this way. Is it someone you know, Aristide?'

'Let me see.' Monsieur Pamplemousse made his way to the balcony. Pommes Frites hurried after him. His hackles rose and he emitted a low growl as he followed the direction of his master's gaze to the street below.

'Aristide!' cried Madame Pamplemousse. 'Where are you going?'

'Out!' said Monsieur Pamplemousse briefly. He looked round for assistance, but Pommes Frites was way ahead of him. When they reached the ground floor he flew out of the lift, and only the fact that the main entrance door was closed prevented him from taking action there and then.

'*Attendez, s'il vous plaît.*' Signalling Pommes Frites to remain where he was for the time being, Monsieur Pamplemousse strode across the rue Girardon to where the man was hovering.

Attack being the best form of defence, he went in with all guns blazing.

'*Salaud!*

'*Cochon* of a macaroni-eating peasant!

'*Allez! Allez!*

'I never wish to see you again . . . *jamais* . . . never!'

All the frustration and fears of the preceding few days erupted.

'And furthermore, when you have your plaster removed tell them to throw away your clothes as well. They offend me.

'You are nothing but a no-good cheap-skate bully of a crook masquerading in a Caraceni suit.

'You are a *maquereau* – a pimp! You are worse than that – you are a failed pimp!'

Each time he thought of something new, Monsieur Pamplemousse emphasised it with a stabbing motion of his right forefinger.

To his surprise, the man suddenly toppled over backwards. As he hit the road his left hand shot towards his top pocket, but Pommes Frites was there before him.

Monsieur Pamplemousse deftly removed a four-inch hat pin and placed the pointed end against the man's ear. 'I could, you know.'

'But you won't.'

'Don't push me,' said Monsieur Pamplemousse in disgust. 'Just don't push me. And I wouldn't stay there if I were you. The *Montmartrobus* is overdue and the driver will be making up time. You are likely to end up as nothing but a bump in the road.'

'*Signore* – all I wanted was to say *grazie . . .*'

'*Grazie?*' Monsieur Pamplemousse paused for breath. 'You wish to thank me? Thank me for what?'

'For finding the girl. We were in charge of her safe-keeping. Think what would have happened to us if we had failed.'

Monsieur Pamplemousse stared down at Il Blobbo as he absorbed what had just been said. He had been assuming all along that the two men had been looking for Caterina for their own immoral purposes. But if Uncle Caputo had charged them with Caterina's safe-keeping while she was away and they had also lost track of her, it put a whole new slant on things. The men would have been in exactly the same position as himself. They, too, would have been going in fear of their lives, and understandably so.

In all probability they would both have ended up suffering the same kind of fate as had the American, William Jackson – a classic case of its kind, demonstrating the extremes of revenge the Mafia took on those members who failed their bosses. People still talked about it.

William 'Action' Jackson, who had blotted his copy-book with Mafia boss Sam Giancana, ended his days hanging from a steel meat hook in a Chicago meat-rendering plant, literally hacked and burned to death, slowly, deliberately and without mercy, by gang members wielding a variety of weapons; ice picks, knives, razors . . . a blowtorch.

Monsieur Pamplemousse stared at Il Blobbo. 'Think yourself lucky,' he said gruffly.

He almost wished now he hadn't mentioned the *Montmartrobus*. It would be a fitting punishment. Il Blobbo by name, ending up as a *blobbo* in the road.

'Aristide!' Doucette stared at her husband as he came back into the room. 'How could you? Attacking a poor defenceless man on crutches. Whatever came over you?'

'I was doing it on behalf of the family of a late attendant on the Palatino,' said Monsieur Pamplemousse. 'Also, a coachload of lathe workers from Nagihuku in Japan. It is unlike the Japanese not to finish off things properly, but that is the way the world is going, I fear.'

'There are times,' said Madame Pamplemousse, 'when I feel I shall never understand you properly.'

'It could have been worse.' Briefly and succinctly, and leaving out certain aspects which experience told might slow down rather than advance the story, Monsieur Pamplemousse brought Doucette up to date, ending with the sorry tale of William Jackson. When he had finished she gave a shudder.

'Such things!'

Monsieur Pamplemousse shrugged. Doucette didn't know the half of it.

Jackson's story hadn't ended there. Shot in the knees, an electric cattle prod stuffed up his rectum and water poured over it for good measure, he had somehow managed to survive for two whole days, setting a record which to date no one had been in a hurry to break.

Photographs of the grim event in its various stages had been distributed as a warning to others not to transgress. He would never forget seeing a copy at the time; even hardened members of the force had gone silent.

'Shouldn't you tell someone?' asked Madame Pample-mousse.

Monsieur Pamplemousse picked up the phone. Doucette was right as usual. There was no reason on earth now why he shouldn't come clean with Jacques.

'I was just about to ring you.' Jacques beat him to it. 'We've got a line on the two men. The short fat one owns a television store in Palermo. On the side he's a specialist in things electronic; phone bugging, safe-blowing . . .'

'. . . solar-powered burglar alarms?' said Monsieur Pamplemousse drily.

'You name it. The one you call Il Blobbo is known as Giuseppi "the Pin" – no prizes for guessing why. Both are known members of the Cosa Nostra. We'll pull them in as soon as we find them, but your guess is as good as mine as to what happens then. You know what it's like. The best we can probably do is make things difficult for them.'

'I don't think either will be bothering anyone for a while,' said Monsieur Pamplemousse. 'If you let me have a copy of the identikit picture and a medical dictionary I will make certain modifications.'

As quickly as possible he gave Jacques an edited version of all that he had told Doucette. He could always fill in the details later.

'Bang goes my dream apartment,' said Jacques when he had finished. 'I was planning to make you an offer when you moved out.'

'It's nice to know who your friends are,' said Monsieur Pamplemousse.

Madame Pamplemousse gave a final flourish of her duster as he put down the phone. 'Did I hear you say the girl has gone back home?'

Monsieur Pamplemousse looked at his watch. 'All being well, she should be in Rome by now.'

'She didn't stay very long. Although if she was how you described her, I imagine *Monsieur le Directeur* won't be sorry.'

'*Merde!*'

'Really, Aristide!' exclaimed Doucette. 'I don't know what has come over you this morning.'

Monsieur Leclercq! He had made one abortive attempt to telephone the Director from the Gare de Lyon the previous evening, but the number had been out of order. Since then he had been so embroiled with his own problems he had quite forgotten to try again.

'He left a message soon after I got in last night,' said Doucette. 'He said to tell you to use his other number next time you called. Ever since his telephone line was cut he's been having to make do with his mobile phone . . .'

'The Director's line was cut?' Monsieur Pamplemousse stared at his wife.

'Apparently it happened soon after you telephoned from the *gendarmerie* and he forgot to tell you the last time you spoke.'

'He forgot to tell me . . .' Monsieur Pamplemousse checked in his diary, then picked up the telephone and dialled. It solved another problem that had been bothering him. He could well understand Il Blobbo wanting to render the Director incommunicado with the outside world – it would have been one of the first things he would have done himself – but leaving him with a telephone had seemed to render the whole operation pointless. Clearly, he thought he had, and equally clearly he had reckoned without Monsieur Leclercq's addiction to gadgets.

'*Monsieur* . . .' But once again Monsieur Pamplemousse had to wait his turn. The Director was bubbling over with his own news.

'Pamplemousse . . . an extraordinary thing happened this morning. I was awakened by a loud explosion. I rushed to the window and was just in time to see pigeon feathers floating down out of the sky. It was an incredible sight – there they were, silhouetted in the light from the rising sun. If only you had been here with your camera.

'What can it mean, Aristide? Do the Mafia have some new method of radio-control at their disposal? Or have they attached some fiendish device to the bird bath?'

'I think, *Monsieur*, it simply means you can come out now. If you go to the window again and look down, I suspect you may find your front door is no longer there.'

While the Director was absorbing this latest piece of information, Monsieur Pamplemousse seized his opportunity.

'Good news, *Monsieur*. Your *petite cousine* is safe. She is on her way home. You can breathe again. In fact, we can all breathe again.'

Quick to jump to the wrong conclusions in times of trouble, the Director was equally prompt in lavishing praise when events took a turn for the better.

Monsieur Pamplemousse wondered how long it would be before the Chief's mind started working in the same direction as his own. The answer came almost immediately.

'You must take Madame Pamplemousse out to celebrate, Aristide. Taillevant, perhaps, or Guy Savoy. I will make the necessary arrangements for this evening. If Chantal can get back to Paris in time we may even join you.'

'It is Sunday, *Monsieur*. They will be closed.'

'You are right. I have lost all track of time.' Monsieur Leclercq tried unsuccessfully to keep the note of disappointment from his voice.

'I did have somewhere slightly less exotic in mind, *Monsieur*.'

'Good. Good. Am I allowed to know where?'

'It is called Mamma Mia's. I believe the owner is a distant relative of Chantal's Uncle Caputo. You are welcome to join us there.'

'You have some unfinished business, Aristide?' The Director sounded slightly nervous again.

'No, *Monsieur*, simply some unfinished *ossobuco*.'

Pommes Frites pricked up his ears at the magic word. If it was anything like the *ossobuco* he had found in the back of his master's car the night before, he couldn't wait. Cold, it had been delicious – although he could have done without the foil – so what it would be like hot didn't bear thinking about! Gastric juices began to flow. Saliva accumulated. He could hardly wait.

'It sounds to me, Aristide,' said Madame Pamplemousse, 'very much as though you are about to make me an offer I cannot refuse.'

'That, *Couscous*,' said Monsieur Pamplemousse, 'is one way of putting it. Although I think Pommes Frites would agree with me, it would be much nearer the truth if you simply said *ought* not.'